T0125297

AN IMPENETRABLE SCREEN OF PUREST SKY

An Impenetrable Screen of Purest Sky

A NOVEL

Dan Beachy-Quick

COFFEE HOUSE PRESS

MINNEAPOLIS

2013

COPYRIGHT © 2013 by Dan Beachy-Quick
COVER AND BOOK DESIGN by Linda Koutsky
AUTHOR PHOTO Stephanie G'Schwind

Coffee House Press books are available to the trade through our
primary distributor, Consortium Book Sales & Distribution,
cbsd.com or (800) 283-3572. For personal orders, catalogs, or
other information, write to: info@coffeehousepress.org.

Coffee House Press is a nonprofit literary publishing house.
Support from private foundations, corporate giving programs,
government programs, and generous individuals helps make the
publication of our books possible. We gratefully acknowledge
their support in detail in the back of this book.

Visit us at coffeehousepress.org

LIBRARY OF CONGRESS CIP INFORMATION
Beachy-Quick, Dan, 1973–
An impenetrable screen of purest sky :
a novel / By Dan Beachy-Quick.
pages cm
ISBN 978-1-56689-341-1 (pbk.)
ISBN 978-1-56689-343-5 (e-book)
I. Title.
PS3602.E24147 2013
2013003661
PRINTED IN THE UNITED STATES
FIRST EDITION | FIRST PRINTING

for Rebecca Beachy

TABLE OF CONTENTS

~~~~~~~~~~~~~~~~~~~~

"I believe in all sincerity that if each
man were not able to live a number of
other lives besides his own, he would
not be able to live his own life."

—PAUL VALÉRY,
"Poetry and Abstract Thought"

"The story is as slender as the thread
on which pearls are strung;
it is a spiral line, growing more and more
perplexed until it winds itself up and dies
like the silkworm in the cocoon.
It is an interminable labyrinth."

—HENRY DAVID THOREAU,
24 March 1842

BOOK ONE

WINTER

CHAPTER 1

THE COCKTAIL PARTIES INCREASED IN NUMBER AND extravagance as the term neared its end. The chair—a man so deeply versed in theory that, caught in the analytic rigor of a minor point in Borges (what kind of shoes the librarians wore . . .), wouldn't notice that the toothpick he kept twirling had some minutes ago lost its shrimp, which, in his half-agitated foot-tapping, he was grinding into paste on the antique rug, and who, once wine enough was in him, talked about Balthus in ways so detailed, so filled with longing ("the cotton-blend of her underwear a pale coral") that he made his colleagues uncomfortable and want to walk away, save at such unrestrained moments, he had the habit of holding whomever he was talking to by the shoulder, and bending his face toward the listener, peering at him over the rim of his glasses, whose thick lenses seemed never to have been cleaned—reserved for this occasion, term over and the night of the winter solstice, the school's old library, lined with leather-bound books. He had initiated the evening by reciting from memory Donne's "A Nocturnal upon St. Lucie's Day," flourishing in one hand a fork with which he kept the meter's time. He recited with eyes closed. The red line of his shut lids magnified by the lenses looked like the scar of a healing wound—a thought that both fascinated and sickened me. Raising the fork higher and higher, his voice gaining emotion, timbre deepening as if he were pulling the last words from some slowly opening sarcophagus in his heart—proof that his beloved truly was interred—he suddenly opened his eyes, eyes so strangely mild and large, bluer than I ever recalled them being, over which his pallid lids seemed like a snow hill in the air, and finished "since this both the year's, and the day's midnight deep is." And at that instant, with a solemn and drawn-out violin accompanied by the cello's deeper sorrow, the chamber musicians began the evening's performance.

I thought he would collapse. But he only brought his hand down, looked curiously at the fork as if he hadn't realized he had been holding it, and not being near a table, slipped it into his jacket pocket.

As the music played, I wandered, looking at the books on the shelf. I wondered if anyone would dare inform the chair that he had misquoted the poem's ending, had transposed *deep* and *midnight,* damaged not only the force of the alliteration, but also the shock there of the double-stress that resounds in the final line like the banging of the bright tongue against the mouth of a dull bell: *day's deep.* I gazed at the books: gilt lettering flame-like against the dark leather bindings. Titles of no interest: *Barbary Captivity in the Late 18th Century, The Worm in Its Element, Pestilence in the Second Kingdom.* Two instructors walked past me holding hands. The music

2

filled the room and, so I thought, subtly reechoed off the plaster ornamentation circling the room's ceiling: autumnal harvest, branch of bare tree, spring grass in which the nightingale nest sat, sunflower, all repeating at regular intervals, and joined together by Pan's repeated face, grinning beneath his horns. Hearing the music once was hearing it twice. My colleagues, people I spend every day talking to or avoiding, seeing in committee or hallway, hearing their footsteps as they walk down the hall to the copier, took on a new aspect; each seemed part of a masque in which his or her own music played, the music of a peculiar drama shifted miraculously but imperceptibly from a strain deep within their own minds to a music in the air, a music all could hear, and hearing, move through, live in, an atmosphere. There are no words to this masque; it is a silent play, a mime. All play themselves perfectly. Even Doris—looking at the arabesque in the carpet into whose swirl her toe encroaches—swaying, anonymous: sea grass in the tide. Pan leered down from the sky. I felt myself blushing: the scent of talc arrived, and the soap underneath the powder, only after Doris has walked by.

I noticed, in my error—that is, my wandering—a book I loved in my childhood, a book forbidden for me to read but which I did read, sneaking into my father's study, reading under his desk. *Wonders and Tales,* by Anonymous. Pages that were the verdant field. Illustrations I would stare at for hours, lines of such minutiae that the detail seemed never to end. I remember an oil

lamp on a desk in an empty room, smoke or steam curling out of the spout, and in the midst of the substance a
woman materializing into form, naked back to me, the
curve of one breast marked by the curve of one line as
she stretched, awakened from how many centuries of
pensive sleep. I couldn't help myself, as the music played,
to reach for it. I felt like a child again, illicit among the
adults, stealing license into that world I would inherit
and longed for, the adult world with its mysterious rites
of longing, its erotic insinuations, that I felt would never
be mine.

I reached for the book, bound in green leather, curious to see it again, to feel it in my hands, expecting, perhaps wrongly, that the page would be a portal back to
my childhood—that perhaps, this being the hidden wish
in all my reading, I still was the child, safe in the dark
beneath my father's desk, that cave in the den, and this
room in which the music played and the people lived so
strangely in their strange lives, lives so separate but connected to my own, was just one of the stories, one of the
tales or the wonders, and that this scene, musicians in an
alcove by the windows, ice sculpture of a fawn melting
into the punch, the secretary drinking wine, her décol-
letage, was an illustration I was looking at too intensely,
entering into it, not noticing when the page became a
world, nor when the illustrator's black-and-white line
became color, became flesh. I reached for the book,
hoping, and my hand knocked against the glass behind
which the books sat on their shelves, glass polished to such

4

clarity, I had not seen it. And only on knocking against it, finding barrier where I thought had been air, did my eye adjust, and I saw, reflected behind me, my good friend looking at me quizzically.

"Should we break it?" he asked. "I brought a little hammer for just such an occasion."

"Yes. Break it," I said.

Olin made as if he were heaving a sledgehammer up from the ground, staggered back with its impossible weight, and then brought it crashing through the glass case. "There," he said. "It's yours." Flourishing his hands outward, the master of an abundant house.

"Thank you, Olin."

We walked off to get a drink; the music ended, the tinkling applause, I like to think, sounded a little like glass falling from its frame to the ground.

CHAPTER 2

A SINGLE GRAIN OF SAND.

In the oyster's mouth—whose whole body is mouth—it becomes a pearl. The bivalve's irritant becomes the lady's jewel.

It is a little world, smooth and round. It can be strung on a thread that, worn against the throat, warms to a blood-heat. It can be set on the golden throne of a ring's setting—a surface milky white, lustrous, but giving back no reflection to the one who brings her hand close to another's face, one who asks to see the ring, and nearing it, sees his own face in silhouette, a shadow slightly distended across the curved surface. It can be kept loose, in a wooden box with a brass clasp, a box lined with black velvet, a mirror on the lid's underside—not unlike the nacre in which it was formed—and a child who plays at "mother," who furtively sneaks into Mother's room, removes with nervous hand the box from the dresser on which it lay, catching a glimpse of herself as she does so in the wardrobe's glass, then running out of the bedroom, down the hall, the pearl crashing against the box's wall, marking the rhythm of her hurried pace.

When she opens the box she sees herself; then she sees the luminescent world against the plush black. A stolen world glows brighter against the night, the night in the box. She picks it up. It weighs almost nothing; isn't cool to the touch, nor warm—it feels as if it has no temperature at all, a sort of absence in the hand. She rolls it around in her palm, mesmerized, the pearl caught briefly in its orbit by the lines in her palm, in which a palmist would read the future: it will be thrown up in the air, love and life, and transformed as it falls. And as if hearing the seer's prediction—this seer who does not exist, or doesn't exist yet—the little girl picks up the pearl between two fingers, picks up her mother's pearl saved for the day when she has enough for a bracelet—and tosses it into the air. The girl meant to catch it, but didn't. It hit the side of her hand and bounced away, fell onto the ground, and rolled across the floor with a noise that sounded like a pencil drawing a dark line on a page, rolled underneath the girl's bed, through the quilt's tassels that brushed against the floor, the pearl rolled through that loose veil into the darkness under the bed, disappeared to the girl's eyes, and then, she heard it as it happened, rolled into the heating register and fell in, one tiny metallic clank revealing its fate. The girl sat up; she had been peering under the bed; she didn't cry, but felt on the verge of tears; she didn't know why, she didn't know how to explain it to herself, but she felt proud.

There is no end of detail to things that don't exist. This pearl?—it had a little mark, a scar almost, like a birthmark, that the jeweler would have drilled through when the time came to pierce through the flaw to make the object flawless. The mother, when she toyed with the pearl, something she did not do often, would unconsciously rub her thumb against that slightest scar, caught in some reverie, some daydream, about her past—a series of thoughts with no connection—she remembered being a little girl with a sore throat, and that her father brought to her bed a cup full of shaved ice about which she thought, when she held it, that the cold rose above the rim as steam rises above a mug of tea, but opposite, and invisible; the mother thought she could see such things. The day of the total eclipse when the silver poplar's shadow turned into flame, and the disappointment after, when the flame was only shadow again—she remembered these things, holding the pearl in her fingers, rubbing the scar with her thumb. There is no end of detail in that world that doesn't exist; it is in this world where detail is a limited resource, this world in which I live. There is a line across which the fact wanders and becomes imaginary, but like the equator, it is an imaginary line—one crosses it and knows something is awry only when the stars rise at night in ludicrous combinations. One remembers how the stars should look, though it is impossible to describe to anyone else—to one's wife: that the bluish star should be closer to the triangle in which two points are more or less reddish (and then pointing), see?, there by the moon! There is a blurry edge, a blurry end, to detail in this world—the ragged moon.

I have a memory, certain memories, in my head. I don't trust them but I need them. When I close my eyes I can call them to mind, a world that unfolds in the darkness of my head, a world my head contains, in which I watch myself inside myself, in which I can even see my own face, eerie mirror of thinking backwards through time. I see myself standing in the door to my father's study, leaning against the jamb; he doesn't know I'm there; he has a scroll and a book open on his desk; the scroll, which he looks at often, his eyes opening wide or narrowing in wonder or in scrutiny, and then he writes in the other book open on his desk; the sound of his writing, of pen on page, I cannot see it, but in my memory I see that sound in lines swirling up from the paper, multiplying as he writes, cocooning him in his own work until I cannot see my father at all, only gray lines moving by their own volition, slowly stilling into form, and my father some strange pupa within the inky silk, becoming something I don't know.

I see I've crossed the equator again. A pearl is made of consecutive layers of nacre, and if one had the patience, and the right tool, one could remove layer after layer—this process might take years—remove the beautiful sheen, ignore the nacre, and find in the very center that irritant in the mouth that caused the unconscious reflex to begin, the helpless instinct that makes of small pain subtle beauty. I would find—

A single grain of sand.

CHAPTER 3

A SMALL GROUP OF FACULTY MILLED IN FRONT OF THE
table where the red wine bottles were placed in two
diagonal rows, and the white in a square formation, three by
three; it looked as if the Pinot Noir were trying to outflank
the Chardonnay; I didn't doubt a professor arranged it so as
some inside joke perhaps only he would understand, a reen-
actment of a battle from the Wars of the Roses. Olin and I
sifted through the loose crowd. Olin drank white and I
drank red; we went to our respective sides. In a voice loud
enough to be overheard Olin said, "Tell me again about
how you met your wife. It was a cocktail party, yes?"

Uncomfortably, "Yes."

"And when you asked her name, she said what? No,
no. You said, 'And what may I call you?'"

"And she said, 'Call me Ishmael.'" I said this with
somewhat less enthusiasm than Olin would have liked.

"Call me Ishmael! That's love at first sight for you
isn't it, Daniel? She really knew how to get her grapples
into ye!" He leered at me cockeyed, one eyebrow raised,
one eye squinted shut, mouth crookedly ajar as if he
were about to spit into a spittoon. The faculty around us
seemed bemused by the performance, recent hires who
still flocked together, and most of whom I didn't know
save by a dim recognition of face.

I have no wife. Olin enjoys, though, sowing the minds of new faculty with blatantly false facts; he hopes to be in near proximity when the truth comes out; in the office when the new rhetoric teacher asks the secretary just what it is my wife does, and the secretary sympathetically, if still curtly, responds, "Daniel? He isn't married." And to the skeptical look in response: "Ask H.R." Olin relishes that moment—he's spoken to me drunkenly about it—when he can see in another's face the instant, save it is an instant that is gradual, as if recognition inside a moment expands the moment past its brief boundaries, the slight tensing of the eyes, the senseless reflex of scrutiny that finds itself investigating a blank wall (the other's face), the brow drawing back and lifting the eyes into a look of bewilderment; and Olin's favorite, the slight flush of the cheek. It is, as he's explained often to me, the way in which knowledge should come. It is the template of knowledge, the archetype, that it comes with shame, and reveals nothing at all. When asked what his pedagogy is by a precocious student, deciding whether or not to take his course on "Information and Deformation," Olin calmly replied, "To fill your mind with dust."

Olin and I sat down in the leather chairs, brass studs lining the arm's curve, ornament but still somehow cruel, whose legs ended in wolf's paws. "What book were you staring at, Daniel?"

"A book I read as a child; one my father said I shouldn't."

"Forbidden fruit, yes. The very best reading a young lad can do."

"I did love it. At night in bed I'd think about the stories. And I'd get scared. But fear made me think more thickly, more fully, so that as I retold the story to myself my mind replayed it. I lost sense of what was real and not real."

"A worthless division."

"Well, maybe. Maybe a necessary one." I paused, just an instant, but one in which the years closed the distance they keep separate. "The room I slept in became alive." I felt embarrassed, but couldn't stop myself, seeing before me what I thought was gone. "I could feel, well— I knew there was a soul in everything, that everything kept making a choice to continue to exist, and welcomed into the world many things that didn't exist but that I could see, a clock that said *now* instead of *tick* or *tock,* other things that spoke to me, that lay next to me, a woman once, she sat on my chest, she was naked, and she told me my future."

"Something similar happened to me last night."

"I'm sure, Olin, it did."

"And what was your future?"

"That I'd be blessed with the chance to know you. 'One day,'" she said, "'you will know Olin.'"

"When I was a boy I could not fall asleep without my mother kissing me. I tormented her with my neediness. But without her kiss, or the extended luxury of her reading me a story, without her presence once again

12

coming into my darkening room, where the magic lantern spun and cast the image of a hunter hunting a wolf that in turning become the wolf hunting the hunter on the walls, I could not risk sleep that, even then, more so than now, I knew was like death. I didn't like to dream. To nightly be given a new world only to find it taken away every morning—a world like our own, sometimes less so, in which those I loved, my mother even, became the monsters they hid inside themselves all day. A fearful thing, yes? It's why I've chosen a healthy insomnia as an adult," his tone ironic but his face hollow, "to avoid sleep as I can, now that my mother is asleep for good."

"The magic lantern . . . you sound as if you grew up in the last century."

"I did." Olin's wit was remarkably dry, to the point at which even I, his good friend, couldn't always tell when he was kidding. He sat in his chair looking at me with some snide innocence, the look of a person who cares that you believe what he is saying so that he can believe it himself.

"I remember when we had to share a room once at a conference. You were asleep in an instant."

"All a ruse. I wanted to protect you from suffering through a night in which I'd ask you to call me Little Olin and tuck me in. Do you know how hard it is to willfully snore lightly for eight hours? It's murder on the nervous system. I woke up exhausted."

My wine was almost gone. "It is hard, Olin, to know when you are telling the truth."

"No, Daniel, it's easy. I'm always telling the truth." He paused. "I mean, I never am. It's hard to tell the difference. I get so confused." At which he winked, stood up, patted me on the shoulder, and walked away, out the room, empty wineglass still in hand.

I took a last sip and followed him, nodding and waving at those I knew, making my good-byes, glancing at the chair playing cards at a table with a stately older man, somewhat portly, dressed in an evening jacket whose lining was scarlet, and whose lips, if I wasn't mistaken, were slightly rouged; a man whom I had never seen before.

The night was bitterly cold. No stars. A kind of brittle fog, unique to our landscape, had settled in. The streetlamps with their cloudlike nimbus lit the walkway. The cold air had fallen to the ground in the minute ice crystals that, at my every step, crunched and dissolved, leaving behind me my dark prints. The night played through my mind, myriad images caught in the chandelier's facets, organized not by time, but by some other order, crystalline.

I walked up the steps and put my hand on the knob, colder even than the night was cold. My father had owned this house; it was the house I grew up in. He had died many years ago; my mother many years before him, when I was still a child.

I opened the door; I'd left it unlocked. And in a pique, for no reason, I shouted out into the empty house, "Ishmael, I'm home."

CHAPTER 4

THE CLOCK STRUCK *NOW* ELEVEN TIMES.

The same mute faces on the wall.

Only one photo of my mother exists. In it her eyes are cast downward. The photo is in black and white, but the photographer hand-colored it: the blush on her cheek, the blue handle of the parasol, the green embankment. As a young boy I would, as Father translated in his study, stand before the photo, bending lower as I neared it, as if I could find an angle from which I could look up and see her eyes staring down at me. My father, catching me crouching, said, "It won't work," and dropped his eyes back down to desk and work.

Now marked the half hour with a single toll.

I walked down the hallway, entered my father's study that is my study now, opened the bottom drawer to the desk, and shuffled through the folders until I found the one I wanted. At night, the mind thinks and the body acts. Or is it the body thinks and the mind acts? Sitting down in the old chair my father sat down in, the chair that's always been old. This body that performs its memory, these hands that open and open the folder, these eyes that see, that read, that read what the mind behind them knows by heart, this heart that pumps the blood, this blood, this ancestral blood in which untold stories circulate, untold tale in the finger, this finger, that touches the page it wrote. Or I wrote. I mean to say this story I didn't write but that I wrote down. This story Father told me. Someone told it to him—or maybe not. Maybe he made it up, a distraction for him more than for me, his son who after his mother died feared sleep, and the dreams in sleep in which his mother, my mother, returned. Maybe he memorized it—the words never altered—so that, as he spoke, sitting in the chair in the corner of my darkened room, his mind could attend to what mattered to him: the language he was learning, an oral language whose basic words and grammar were translated by a missionary two hundred years ago and whose helper had written down, in the phonemes of the romantic alphabet, though tainted by the Latinate habits of his ear, a story told by an elder of the tribe, written on a scroll, titled in Spanish, *Mito de Creación,* a thick roll of paper my father found in a box in a country library as he travelled through England as a young man, bought for a few pence, and whose academic life, when I was a boy, and until he died, was devoted to translating. It was a task he never finished, much to his regret. I might be wrong. Perhaps every word of the story he spoke he vividly saw, escaping into the same story he gave me for my escape, and to change a word would destroy the world he was conjuring. Either way, he sat in the darkest corner of my room, so that his voice seemed to come from the night itself, the night lulling to sleep the child unwilling to go to sleep, the night telling its story.

After my father died, the very day he died, I sat at this desk and wrote down that story word for word. I wrote it down in my illegible scrawl and took it to my room, lay down on my bed, and in the dim light read it, and read it again, over and over again, until the window began to grow light. The alarm clock went off at 5:45. There had been an earthquake in Guatemala, a powerful earthquake felt in Belize and Panama; only one person had died.

I took the pages to my room, undressed, and got in bed. The wine tugged my mind toward the still house's familiar silence. I read the story.

After the giant removed his heart and buried it in the ground his eyes gradually grew smaller and smaller until he seemed to have no eyes at all. He did still have eyes, but they were no larger than pinpricks, smaller than the eyes of a mole, as small as a spider's eyes, and let in so little light that the giant was mostly blind. He couldn't tell when it was night or day and so he stopped sleeping. He couldn't walk without running into trees or tripping over ridges or falling down in rivers. The giant just sat down and didn't move. He sat so long that moss grew on him. Grass grew on the moss. Trees in the grass: an aspen grove. He seemed dead but he was not dead. When the wind pushed through the aspen and the leaves made a riverlike music the giant would hear it, some nerve would awaken, and though he had no heart, from his pinprick eyes a tear would fall, so thin and meager that the wind that caused it would also take it away. People who passed the giant thought he was only a hill whose stony crest was pink as skin. Their parents and their parent's parents had walked by the hill many times, had carted their goods down the road that curved around the giant, and in all their memory that hill had only ever been a hill. But the birds knew. Whether they could hear his breath, or feel the slightest twitches of muscles that sometimes sent a leaf spiraling down from a branch in midsummer, or sense beneath his head the hum of his thinking, no one can say—so there were no nests in the aspen trees. But the people didn't notice this either. To the sudden absence of birdsong at the hill when they walked past it the people all were deaf.

It was at the foot of this hill that the people of the village built their schoolhouse.

The story has no end I know. It has no end because my father never told me an end. As a boy I would ask him to tell me the rest.

The voice from the dark would say, "The rest is in your dreams." And then from out the dark my father would step and walk from my room.

It was not a dream I ever had.

I read the story once, twice, I read the story. In the room, my winter room, I could smell the scent of an apple—why is that? I could smell an apple as if an apple were asleep in the old wardrobe, dreaming about me. I turned out the light. The phosphorescent glow in my eye, the bright white-purple glow behind my lid—do you see it?—doesn't it look a little bit like an apple tree in bloom? Don't you see it?—

I asked who?—

And fell into a fitful sleep.

CHAPTER 5

none of the schoolchildren could explain
they opened their eyes into circles

they found the desks pushed against the walls
when they walked in the schoolroom's door

and on the old rutted wood
near the center of the room

—they saw a single pearl

*

the giant's heart is

at fault in the fault

*

my father at his desk, looking up:

there is no difference in this
language between

the definite article and the indefinite
"The" or "A"—there is no way to tell

he started crying

"And it's the first word written down here on the
page"

holding up a page marked by a
musical note

✸

Olin cleaning the chair's glasses with the end
of his shirt and then kissing him

I stood in the room, reading
the old book, a cut on my finger

left my fingerprint in

blood
on the page

✸

A whale sounds down in the ocean.
Eye as small as a foal's. I know
he sees me watching him

the white whale. There is a tarred
rope tangled around him, but
it does not slow his descent.

Placid as ice as it forms
within the element of its
own composition.

There is a man in the mouth.
That man is me.

✳

I was glad to be hungover when the sun woke me up.
There is no doubt the hangover is real—except when I
try to explain it to myself. I drank, I walked home, I
read. I had many dreams that I dreamed. And now I have
this pain behind my eyes, it has a shape, a circle or an
orb, it isn't large—this pearl that is the pain in my mind.

CHAPTER 6

I POURED MYSELF A CUP OF COFFEE AND WALKED DOWN the hall to the study. My father had lined the walls with cork to quiet the noise of the street. He feared that the intermittent voices of women discussing their children, of children furtively whispering their cruel taunts of the local man who, half-crazed and half-drunk, knocked on doors and yelled into houses, "Encyclopedias for sale!" but who had no books to sell, of vendors selling their wares on the streets, pushing a cart with bells dangling from the handle, "Ices, ices, ices and treats," a song in refrain syncopated by the tinkling notes, the man who every day chose a different corner from which to proclaim, in stentorian tones, "The world has ended, and it's gonna rain, the world has ended, and it's still gonna rain, get out, it's calling, get out, it's too late to repent, the world has ended, and here's the proof," at which point he would sing hymns from the old hymnal, his eyes closed, in a profound bass that at its lowest notes seemed not to be heard so much as felt, of daily conversations, of men discussing the derby, of the poor woman who as she walked talked to herself, "It couldn't have been different, it could have been different" over and over again, just as the young girl wandered with the daisy in her hand, "He loves me, he loves me not." Father said the slightest intonation overheard could destroy a day's work; a single word could make worthless hours of concentration. This language, he'd tell me when I'd listen, couldn't be translated by simply referring to a dictionary; there was no dictionary. But the difficulty was far greater, he claimed. One couldn't, he couldn't, nor could anyone, create a dictionary of this language, write down the various parts of speech, what transliterated words referred to object or person or action or comparison or indication or conjunction or division in our own language; this language was rooted, if such a word can be used in this case, in a profound instability, in which no single word ever stilled into definition of one single thing. Not only could one not tell apart the definite article from the indefinite, that sound that word is, slightly altered by intonation, extended by breath, could become not only a word referring to a bird, but *a-bird-that-nests-on-the-open-bare-ground* and also, simultaneously, so my father claimed, *the-fragile-rock*. It could drive me mad. I could be driven mad by it. He would stare down at the old transcription, written on a scroll rather than bound, as if the language were a landscape instead of a book; two stones held the scroll open, stones rubbed smooth by the ocean, large as my father's hands; he would stare down at the words written on the paper, and then close his eyes, for hours close his eyes, and do nothing at all, write down nothing. He kept by the scroll's side a sheaf of paper on which was printed musical staff. It is a song, a music. You have to hold the whole music in your mind to hear the story, it has to be sung to be said, and if I write down a

24

word plucked out from the tune the entire song falls apart, everything is lost, it's all blank, the ear is blank. You must hear it to see it, and when you see it, you can write down some equivalent. He would talk to me, when he talked to me of his work, in the first person and the second person, so that listening to him absorbed me into him, or him into me, the division between father and son, him and me, I and you, falling prey to the same indeterminate quality of the language he was translating. He didn't, my father, translate the myth into words, but into a musical notation of his own composition, a notation made of musical notes, other marks to distinguish rhythm, wavelike lines rolling upward or downward through the staff to mark intonation and, should he be able to complete his thoughts for the day, one word he'd write on top of the page, *white* or *cloud* or *water* or *then*. "I have discovered today that *and* is the same word as *or*; it is the most complex word I've understood." He didn't look victorious when he said this to me; he sounded defeated. He held out his hands as if he were offering me something. And when a word would break through the room's cork-lined silence, it would be gone, all of it, the whole music, world's melody; when through the walls rumbled the awful words "The world has ended," my father opened his eyes, and in his look was the proof.

CHAPTER 7

I LEARNED TO BE A QUIET CHILD.

I learned to be a quiet child. These are the words with which, now many years ago, I began the novel I'm still writing. In the mornings, it is my work. I don't show it to anyone; I don't tell anyone I'm working on it. I am, in certain ways, embarrassed. I began with ambitions the very first sentence ended; a novel whose taproot dug down into fairy tale, but from that root, split, rhizome-like, erupting out of the ground in shoots and leaves that seem wholly unconnected to their source, different leaves, different worlds, but should one be able to trace the fine thread-roots over their strange coursing, the disparate would be seen as whole, a many and a one, the multiple world.

But what I write about is myself, my childhood, my friends, dinner parties, music, the bewildering dazzle of social hierarchies, artists I know and the art they make, my father's work. I wanted to write a different world; I write the small, cunning world I am. It is a limit I have resigned myself to, my life. The page is a curious mirror one polishes with oneself to see oneself clearer, but the polishing, as it brings the surface to a sheen, also warps it, alters the image into beauty that does not exist, or cruelty that does not exist, except latent, a virus or a seed

dormant in the personality, awaiting the right condition
to spring into life, to viruslike infect the cell, to weed-
like run rampant through the field, but the only element
of life is life, this life I lead, in which the pages I write
become the fallow field waiting to be turned over,
where the sentences are the plough's edge turning up
the sod into sillion's dark shine. This work—I cannot
seem to stop it, though I would like to—this effort at
consciousness that dismantles itself into uncertainty,
changing facts into myths, self-myths, so that reading
back through the pages, the hundreds of pages, gives me
back to myself in altered form; did I seduce the student
in my office when she came in the early spring, here
where the northern latitude keeps night arriving early,
asking about Melville's *Encantadas*?; did I speak to her
about enchantment, about song and place, about the
dinner party in the summer air, tents lit by torches, in
which I saw the island tortoise walk into the dark
woods, *memento*★★★ in burning letters on its back?; did I
put my hand on her knee, and run my hand up beneath
her skirt? What I have made up about myself has so
insinuated itself into my imagination it acts as fact;
imagination embraces fact, subsumes it, as an amoeba
will swallow itself to end its hunger, and then sated,
split in two, and make of itself another. I once ended a
semester's class, after Ishmael, another orphan, had been
rescued by the devious-coursing *Rachel,* by saying "A
book begins by defining 'Who I am'; it ends by asking
'Who am I?' We are allergic to the world; consciousness

is an allergic reaction to the fact of the world; it is our understanding that is a form of irritation, a rewarding irritation, and we think, because we think, we have accomplished something noble, something valorous, that we can say what it is something means; but it is just a symptom of the allergy, the mind trying to rid itself of itself, of what enters it by casting it back out, words for world."

I know that I ended a class with these exact words. It is recorded in Book III, Chapter VI on page 147 of the manuscript.

MOTHER DIED IN CHILDBIRTH. SHE HAD BEEN CONFINED TO her bed for months; I found her fingerprint in the dusting of talc on her boudoir's cluttered surface; I bent my face low and blew the dust away. She was my mother who died in childbirth. Altering the sentence cannot alter the fact. I found her fingerprint in the dust and blew it with my breath away; I did this when she was still alive. It was then I was a child.

I don't remember much, which is why my memory is so accurate: one cast-iron pinecone on the metal chain clicked upward while the other clicked down so I knew the minutes were passing even when the bird didn't—springing out her house's door—sing. I remember the dark rooms of the house lit up by lantern light, a yellow light that warmed the darkness, revealed the darkness, more than it countered it, removed it; but we owned no lanterns. My father read a book. When Mother screamed from upstairs and Father went up to listen through the door, I walked over to his desk. Spine-cracked, the book lay flat. He had underlined one sentence on the page, underlined it over and over again—"It is very unhappy, but too late to be helped, the discovery we have made, that we exist"—with such repetitive force he had cut through the page with the pen's nib and crossed out a sentence on the page below. I don't remember reading the sentence; I couldn't read then. I remember turning the page over, and seeing underneath the dark line cut precisely *through the words, severing them in half,* "~~It is but a choice between soft and turbulent dreams. People disparage knowing~~"— *but I couldn't yet read.*

My father came back and looked at me; I was sitting at his desk, looking at the book he had just been reading, holding his pen in my hand. For many years I have tried to write a description of his face; once, in the back of a car driving through the countryside, being chauffeured to the estate of a wealthy patron of the college, and seeing three trees on the roadside, trees through which the wind was blowing and knocking from within them their cottony seed, I saw once again my father's face, saw him looking at me, and, taking out my journal from my case, tried to draw what I had always failed to describe; it was a likeness I was pleased with until, the car hitting a rut in the road, I drew a line through his eye. His was a face that could not be described; there was a line between his eyes that cut through them. He looked at me as if I were him. "You know it already. Your mother has died." My father, he was not an unfeeling man; he spoke with no emotion. I can hear his voice now. Emotion—it stops when it enters grief's true realm. The bird sang out the hour.

I had a little sister and no mother; my father had a daughter and no wife. My sister was not well. The doctor handed her to my father and said she did not have long to live, that my father should name her, but he wouldn't. He said he wouldn't give her a name. He simply took her from the doctor—a man who seemed to me to disappear at that very instant, as if in being in such proximity to death and life made him less than material, subject to laws other than natural laws—and began pacing through the house, through the long hours left in the night, until the morning grayed the sky into vision, humming some tune that is no song, and I followed him, humming the same tuneless notes, echoing his steps with my steps, running my fingers along the walls of the house until, the sun breaking the horizon's line, he stopped his dark song, stopped his wandering, and said, "It's done."

It was my sister.

CHAPTER 9

THE BOX WAS EMPTY.

The girl put the empty box back on her mother's dresser and went back to her room. She got down on her stomach and inched under the bed; her legs stuck out.

The girl thought about the pearl in the duct. She could see it in her mind, patient in the dark, a little world around which the hot wind blows. She could be as patient as the pearl; she was a pearl herself; her mother called her "my little pearl"; her name was Pearl. On her stomach, under the bed, blanket's bright fringe dimming the light, the girl knew what it was the pearl felt like.

She knew that the metal grating led downward into the house; she could picture it. She could see the duct slope downward and expand, she saw the duct beneath the house was larger than the house, widening into the earth beneath the foundation, opening into the inner ocean, the ocean inside the world where the islands are still uncharted, where there was no map, where the stone faces stood sentry looking for ships, statues whose eyes were pearls; she could see the pearl in the sea, falling down in the water, swayed only slightly by the current as it blew. She saw it falling, saw on the ocean's bed the oyster with unhinged mouth open, awaiting the pearl's return. Pearl was in the ocean too: blanket's blue fringe

32

sealike swaying surrounding her. It was nice to drown; necessary. Then she could hear the voices. The voices in the water. One of the voices was her mother's.

It came up through the ductwork, her mother's voice in the kitchen. She was talking but no one was there with her. It was the old story, the story her mother told: *The giant took out his heart and buried it.* Her mother's voice told her the story from the ocean's bed where in the water all the stories tell themselves over and over again. Pearl fell with the pearl, lullaby of her mother's voice. The box was empty, but it was empty in another world, a world in which the night sky was starless as was the inside of the box, night's black velvet. That was a world in which everyone was asleep. That was the world everyone slept in, the world before the turbulent dreams began.

Mother's voice stopped speaking before Pearl heard it stop. In her dream her mother's voice was the ocean. The long current was the pull on her legs, it was the current, until the ocean stopped being the ocean, when the blue water became again the blue fringe, when she woke up. Her mother pulled her out from under the bed.

Pearl turned around and looked up. Her mother was holding in her hand the box, lid open.

The box was empty.

BOOK TWO

SPRING

CHAPTER 1

THE FURNACE SHUTTING OFF SOUNDS LIKE A WAVE RUSH-
ing under itself as it draws back into the ocean. That
sound, which leads to its own absence, woke me up
before the alarm went off. Spring morning, window a
crack open, gray-blue light limning the horizon that
isn't, after all, so far away. Dreams about the weather.
Drops of rain like pearls on rose leaves, last year's old
buds withered, like burnt-out suns above them, unable
to evaporate the dew. Then the silence in the house wasn't
silence anymore: wood's small cracks and creaks, the
sound from the first floor as of a squeaky hinge. Then
the alarm's click before the radio's voice kicks on. A
poet, the reporter reports, studying volcanoes for a new
book, disappeared on a small island in Japan. He left the
island's only inn early in the morning, a day-pack and a
walking stick his only equipment. The volcano wasn't
large, though it is active. Police found his footprints at
the trailhead, but soon lost them in the heavy forest. The
path leads to the crater, where noxious fumes leak out of
the mouth. Investigators are certain the poet did not fall
into the volcano. There is no explanation for their certainty. A steeper path on the mountain's back has yet to
be explored. Night came on before the searchers could
conclude their search. The steep path leads from the

edge of the bed, down the stairs, to the study where the same pages wait, some full of words, some empty. The story has lost its order, the story I am writing, this story of my life. Emerson thought the mind's nature was volcanic; my father was the first person to tell me this. A rock falls into the eye and becomes molten in the mind and memory cools it back into the rock first seen. It alters when it reemerges, but one cannot tell the difference. It looks the same, but we are imagining it. Memory is igneous more than ingenious, igneous, and like granite, intrusive, heaved up within oneself, the whole range of one's life, mountains' forbidding height looming over the plains where one lives, mountains formed by the life already lived, but toward which one is always walking, one's own past ahead of him, seeking the improbable path already forged, this path back through oneself, this path we call the present tense, which becomes the continental divide when the tense shifts and the path is lost, path from which the walker emerges only to turn around and see the peaks pulled up by his feet, and the snowy pass, and alpine heights, where those stranded sometime must feed on themselves to survive, where sometimes, through the icy crust, the crocus blooms. White hills of pages, there you are—on the flat desk. And only when I sit down do I notice a black beetle upside down, rowing his legs against the air. Then I knew the poet fell into the volcano's crater, despite the investigator's assurance. There is nowhere else to fall.

CHAPTER 2

B LANK PAGES . . . IN THEM, AS A WATERMARK SEEN WHEN held up to the window's light, hides the Delphic oracle, *Gnothi Seauton,* save it isn't the window's light that makes the command visible. *Certain scenes the book prescribes for itself, a kind of fate. Critics disdain the "episodic" but it is an ancient decree the writer, when honest, is helpless to deny.* Two sentences and the morning's writing feels done; and those words not even fictive, not furthering the plot, what of plot there is—criticism masking cryptic doubts. What more there is to write is hidden in what is already written, those pages already filled that, face-down on the desk, are as blank as the unwritten pages awaiting the next words.

The hour stretched out before me, longer than itself.

Essays to grade sat in a folder in my bag; notes to review before teaching; it all whispers and waits on the edge where time becomes time again, when memory returns to its confines as a debtor returns to prison; the obligatory day is the turnkey, locking memory away.

My father's name was Allan; my mother's name was Maria. These are facts I keep to myself. I think of them as Father and Mother; those are the names by which they live in me, names that are not names at all, simply these earthly types the gravestones mark: *father, wife.*

Allan was a man who died after destroying his career in crazed pursuit of translating a holy text; Father was the man who on his deathbed forgot my name, the name he gave me, and who said, looking at me directly, "You've been a good son." The leaves of the poplar clicked against the window as they did then, a gentle coaxing to pay attention not too closely. The white underside of the poplar leaves—

Father didn't want a funeral, but his mother-in-law refused him; she already thought he was deranged. She arrived by train, carrying in both hands ponderously in front of her a portman-teau stitched together from an old tapestry: a red bird with a flame-like tail perched on a water bowl in the middle of a flower garden, and curving from underneath the bag, slightly frayed, a sundial complete with shadow; the time was two o'clock.

"Take this, Daniel," she said, handing it to me, a bag I couldn't lift by myself. All my family save my aunt called me Danny; but my grandmother believed in the propriety of the speaking of proper names as much as she betrayed that propri-ety in her actions. I dragged her bag after me as I followed her down the hall. "Allan, Allan," she sang out, almost as if singing a song to coax a child from his hiding spot. "Allan . . ." Her voice wandered through the house ahead of her, spreading out through the rooms she had yet to bodily enter, filling in every empty space with her overabundant self. I silently dragged time down the hall after her. "Allan, I'm here, I'm here to help." Stopping to look down at me, "Now, go along and get me a cup of lemon tea, my feet are killing me, from travel, you know this

about me," and as if she hadn't been speaking to me at all, picking up her address to my father mid-sentence, "Allan, travel wrecks my nerves. I feel faint, Allan. Allan, I feel—" and then she stopped talking. Not because Father had emerged from his study, but because she saw, in the middle of the living room, the fire in embers behind them, the two coffins.

"We don't have any tea." Father had appeared.

"No, you don't," she said in a voice of deep concern, and, hearing me inch up behind her with her massive bag, sat down upon it, giving me only a moment to escape being sat upon myself, and started crying, not loudly, but silently, the most quiet I ever remember her being. She cried and looked at the coffins. Minutes passed. Father wandered back to his office, back to his desk, the scroll open on it, window open despite October's chill.

She looked at me blankly. "It's so small."

I looked at the dark box in which my sister lay. "She is small," I said, and put my arm on her knee, and stood beside her while she cried. Everything was so quiet. I could hear my father's pen scratch the page from his study down the hall.

There was also the scratch from my own pen, sitting there at my desk, which was his desk then. There in the blank pages hid the old oracle, *know thyself,* impossible decree. It was Aunt Leonie who, sickly on her bed when we visited in the summer, drank lemon tea and ate cookies, asking after the gossip of the town. But Aunt Leonie is not my aunt, just a character in another book whom I want to be a character in mine. My grandmother was Clarel; she drank instant coffee; she was grief-struck by her daughter's death—the word, I think, is *siderated*. The muses, I thought as I put the written pages on a pile and put the pile away, tell lies as if they were the truth, and tell the truth when they like. Memory is the mother of the muses.

As I grabbed my bag to go to work I thought about Clarel's bag, a bag as large as I was at the time, a bag I could have curled up within and gone to sleep—it would be as if I had never been born. I thought about the bag, and what the bag implied; that somewhere, at an angle almost discernible, there sat in the sky a bright sun, a sun that never moved, whose light cast down on the garden also grew a shadow on the sundial. It was two o'clock. And written on the sundial, in letters finer than the thread could show, were these words: *The Hour Knows / What Shadows Show.*

CHAPTER 3

THE DEW ON THE GRASS, SOMEONE HAD WALKED ACROSS it, footprints that looked like shadows. His path marked by the dew being removed with each step became the dew-wet marks that darkened the cement, each step less distinct as the wet soles dried, soon just a circle-of-heel behind a circle-of-toe, and then only the toe, fainter in the middle so that the print seemed cloven, as of a deer, and then smaller, a goat—the old god Pan leaping back into the trees whose leaves his pipes had coaxed into unfurling. The man walked away into nothing—the same direction I was walking in—another self who had watched me through the window as I wrote, a previous self, some alternate version, or someone not yet to be, the impossible self who could have been, who is and isn't at once, not troubled by memory by writing memory down, the dew on the grass, those pearls of dew he stepped through, the only evidence he exists outside of me. A thought leaves no print; leaves only the print of word in ink on page. A footprint so mocking as it disappears; you follow what cannot be followed, it says. My own absence wandered out ahead of me walking, thinking the thoughts I'd forgotten to think or cannot think—that the morning's writing had cast me out ahead of myself and that I was impossibly, unexpectedly late, following myself to work, under the tree-lined walkway, where the leaves had only recently unfolded from their buds.

The path went by the statelier houses on the outskirts of the college, keeping a respectful distance; the grandeur could be seen, but not the lives inside it. In the early morning, earlier than this hour, a light in a bedroom window would sometimes switch on, a yellow square in the dawn. Sometimes I could see the shadow of a woman in the yellow square. I often walked the same path as a child, by myself, or with my father as he walked to school, reciting to me the lecture he soon would recite to his students, looking at the notes written in his Victorian hand on the yellowing square of notebook paper, forgetting the young boy walking beside him wasn't a student, "The rose must be told it is sick, *O rose, thou art sick!*, it doesn't know it for itself. The worm that loves it, whose secret love destroys it, flies in the storm in the dark. The worm is winged, a fact which we seldom imagine and must not forget. It is easy to hate the worm, but the worm, more than the rose, is who we identify with. Students (and here he'd look up, as if expecting to see his class, and seeing only the apple tree in bloom on the rise, and then looking down at me looking up at him, would lower his voice, and continue), the worm is invisible, it flies in the dark, it cannot be seen, its love is secret, and it finds in the rose her bed of crimson joy. That bed is deep in her heart. The heart is a crimson bed, the place of consummation both erotic and spiritual. The rose does not

44

know it's sick; the poet must tell her. The poet must tell the rose that in her there lives a worm, a worm that loves her, and that its love will kill her. The poet must tell her, as the professor must tell you, the worm is in you, it does not kill from hate, but destroys in love, it was inside her, no one told her, it—" and then Father stopped, the apple tree was before us, and he looked up into it, the pale-pink almost-white blossoms filling the entire canopy, the pale petals all the paler against the dark branch, and some petals falling, as if the tree were a cloud, pale little petals, as pale as faces in winter. "Remind me, Daniel, of this apple tree tonight. I need to think about it more—for the translation." He looked sad. We kept walking, but the lecture was over.

Father left me at the door to Trillbyrne Hall, the building in which the English department had been housed since the college's founding. The architecture was neoclassical, but with certain eccentric touches: chimera as caryatid, and atop the cupola, a windvane in the shape of a whale, the letter *S* carved out of the iron for an eye. Every direction the whale looked was *south*—a whale is always diving down. I remember walking back along the path, thinking about the rose, the sick rose. I cried as I walked. And when I got home, I wrote on the little notepad kept by the phone in the front hall, *Remember the Apple Tree* in a child's blocky script. Then I went into my father's office, pulled my favorite book from the shelf, the book I was not allowed to read, and sat in the cave under his desk reading: *The faeries sleep inside flowers. They sleep all day and all day the buds are closed. But at night the blossoms open, and the queen of the faeries scratches a line in the earth where a river will flow. The river flows to a house where a woman is soon to give birth. The faeries secrete themselves into the room; no one sees them because they hide in people's shadows. It is hard for them to stay so still in the shadows; staying still takes all their effort. The faeries wait to steal the baby, to put her in the boat made of leaves, to carry her to the faerie land, where she too will sleep in flowers—for faeries want nothing more than to raise a human child for themselves. And when the child is grown, when she can walk and talk and think, when she begins to suspect the faeries are faeries, that she has been stolen; just before she asks who her mother and father are, where they are, the faeries take her on a long journey to the volcano that marks the center of their world; the queen commands them to do this. They walk beside the child as she walks to the crater's mouth. The faeries say they must all jump in, that the volcano is a doorway into another world, the world in which the child's mother and father live, waiting for their child to return. The faeries say they found her as a baby on the lip of the volcano's mouth and rescued her; they say they've been through the volcano many times. And when the girl jumps in the faeries jump with her, fall with her until the heat becomes too great, and then they unfold their wings, and the girl looks up at them as she falls, floating in the hot air . . .*

I turned the corner where the apple tree used to stand— cut down many years ago, and in whose place the saplings never seemed to be able to grow. Bag heavy enough with books to make my hand ache. For some time now, I realized, the dew-wet footprints were again on the path.

Some scents in spring burst forth with such fragrance to encounter them is as if to run into a person, but instead of collision, you step wholly into the body of the other and live for a while inside her. Only she is no *her,* only the body of the lilac's scent, which never fully diffuses through the air. It is a scent I try to avoid, a moment I try to avoid, this reverie inside the lilac's odor, this scent that is a presence without a body, a touch more subtle than physical touch, that evokes memory from nothingness, memory so vivid as to be felt in the nerves, to live again that which cannot be lived again, love lost and the lover's lost touch, she who I let leave; it is a scent that grows sickly when one lingers in it not moving, stays in it remembering what cannot help but be remembered, making love in the bedroom with the windows open while the hailstorm violently stormed, destroying the garden, the pea plants' threadlike tendrils pulled from the twine around which they'd twined, shredding the leaves from the trees; and it is never "one" who steps into the lilac's scent and forgets to keep walking, it is always me. I looked down. There were his footprints, whoever he is. One foot after the other until, once again, growing smaller as they progress, the prints disappear.

I thought to myself: I must remember to tell Father about the apple tree.

Then, very quietly, I said to myself her name—

CHAPTER 4

"LYDIA, MEET DANIEL." OLIN TURNED TO ME WITH A look exaggerated in meaning. "Daniel, meet Lydia."

We exchanged our awkward hellos. Olin rushed glasses of wine into our hands, "Empty hands, empty hands, the devil's playthings."

"I think, Olin," Lydia said, "it is *idle* hands."

"Idol hands? Really?" Olin's voice in its fullest mock sincerity. "Well, the human hand is venerable, certainly. I can understand the desire to idolize it. I could sign up for that religion. Such a nicer object to kneel in front of than, say, a cross. Idol hands."

I looked at Lydia. "He is hopeless, you know."

"No asides, Daniel, no asides. I hear them all. Tonight is no Restoration drama. No monologues in the middle of the room in the midst of others. No invisible walls. Tonight we get to talk. Here are my two favorite colleagues (if, Lydia, I can claim a physicist as a colleague—I think I can) and more than a bottle of wine for each of us, carefully chosen to suit our personalities, wine with a personality itself—all we have to do is drink it to be brilliant conversationalists." Olin looked to each of us in turn, an imploring look, as of a fawn to her mother. "And I'm not hopeless. Or I am. I forget which." A hand on each of our shoulders, Olin guided us into the living room, sat us down in facing armchairs, a fire not casting off too much heat, whose flames ringed the edge of our glasses with orange light, and backing away, "The coq au vin calls me back to him. Occupy yourselves with each other and don't despair, I'll return."

I looked at Lydia looking at the fire, and then I looked at it myself. "A physicist?"

"Yes, it's true." She paused as if, I thought, deciding whether or not to go on, knowing that the next word might incline the conversation to that inevitable sense of confession, helpless as gravity, of unfolding oneself in words to another person hardly known, an act in some ways more intimate than sex, more erotic, denying the retreat to embrace when words fail, no means of communication beyond what can be said that, unlike physical intimacy, is not a knowledge of another person by moving the body to the pleasures the body opens, but the opposite, knowing her only by what she tells of her life, some glimpse as strangely private as the blue vein in her neck seen just beneath the outspread veil of her hair when she looks away at the fire, or the pulse of her wrist when, reaching for her glass, the cuff of her sleeve withdraws. There was a magazine on the table between the chairs with an owl on the cover. She opened it. Two yellow eyes, one on each page, beak in the gutter—the perfect symmetry of the owl's face creased, as if it could be folded in half. And then Lydia unfolded each of those pages, lengthening away from each other, two, three, four times, until the pages extended almost past her own arms' reach; sitting in her lap, outstretched arms holding the last feathers by their tips, spread out the whole wingspan of a great horned owl in flight. A fork dropped in the kitchen; Olin uttered some curse I couldn't quite hear. As Lydia began folding the wings back upon themselves she spoke: "It wasn't what my father expected; not at all. He was a musician, a cellist. I grew up playing the violin. I even composed some pieces. He had the highest hopes of my being a prodigy."

"It sounds as if you were."

"I loved it, but I didn't have to *think* about it, and as I grew older, I wanted to think, to struggle, to not understand. Music was second nature, almost innate. And so in college I turned from music to astronomy—"

"The celestial spheres—" I interrupted.

"Yes. The music of the spheres." She took a sip of wine. "Astronomy led me to physics, and here I am."

"As simple as that?"

"Well, it's not *that* simple. It is," she paused, glancing at me, "musical. My father couldn't understand that, and I couldn't find a way to explain it to him. It is music that taught me how to think about the universe."

"The 'universe'—I have to admit, it sounds so implausibly lofty. Your job is thinking about the universe. I find that a little, well, intimidating."

"Don't. It's your job, too—isn't it? Thinking about the universe?"

"I read books. I make my students read the books I read. And then we talk about them." I felt bad at the sound of my voice, the defeat in it.

She looked at me for a moment, and tilted her forehead toward me just slightly as she spoke. "Exactly the same." Small awkwardness: she kept rubbing her thumb in circles underneath the glass that now empty chimed low with the motion. "I disappointed my father."

"Mine disappointed me." Olin came back before I could elaborate on what I didn't mean to say. I stood up as if I hadn't spoken the words that had just left my mouth.

"Dinner, kids, is served." A bottle of wine open between two candles whose light, after leaving the fireside, seemed to end in needle points. The chicken dished on the plates already, a thick burgundy stew steaming, and on the table, a baguette, and asparagus in a scalloped bowl. We all sat down, and Olin, picking up his glass, initiated the dinner, "To friends of mine becoming friends to each other." We clinked and drank; a moth flew in circles within the shade of the floor lamp.

"What are you teaching this term, Olin?" Lydia asked, gracefully letting the intimate thread of the earlier conversation drop.

"I am teaching nothing disguised as an upper division class on philosophy of language."

"Olin has mastered, so he tells me, the ability to riddle a student with her own questions in such a way that the student feels more intelligent for knowing nothing at all."

"What a skill, Olin," Lydia said, "you are a veritable Socrates."

In full seriousness, deadpan, "It has been said before,

exactly so, dear Lydia, on a number of evaluations. It is lucky, I should add, that Phaedrus and Meno didn't get a chance to fill out evaluations; Socrates, I can attest, might have found it hard to get tenure. He was lazy, too, about publishing. But Lydia, enough about me, no more talking about me, I bore myself, I have bored myself for years, and see that boredom reaching into the future; I am just as Dickinson has it: *It might be more boring without the boringness*; that is exactly me."

"That *is* exactly you, Olin," I answered, "save Dickinson's was 'more lonely without the loneliness.'"

"'*Loneliness*,' that's right. I always forget there's a difference." Olin paused, struck by himself. "And Lydia, what does the semester hold for you?"

Lydia put her fork and knife down on the china. "I don't have any teaching at all. They've given me the semester for research and writing."

"And what are you working on?" I asked.

"Inflationary theory." Lydia looked slightly abashed.

"It sounds awful," Olin said, "like doomsday economics or the scientific study of balloon tying."

"I know, it does sound awful. And I am very bad at tying balloons into animals; I tried once, at a niece's birthday party; I made a poodle that looked like a spider that made a five-year-old cry before it popped. No, it is a thinking back to the moment of the Big Bang, that first instant in which the universe exploded from a singularity to an infinitely expanding everything. There are some theorists, and I guess now I am one of them, who suspect that multiple other universes began at the same time, each infinite in scope just like ours, but perhaps formed so differently as to have entirely other natural laws. These universes are, some say, the multiverse; they aren't wholly separate from one another. There are realms, theoretically, where one universe touches and merges into the other, where the 'laws' collide, a genuine chaos that causes the birth of another universe. It's that collision I'm considering." She looked a little flushed, seemed a bit out of breath; she didn't make eye contact with anyone, as if she had just divulged an embarrassing, half-thought-out superstition.

"Gravity working in reverse?" I offered. "Purple skies? Warm ice?"

"Well, sort of, but no, not at all. The difficulty, I find, in trying to explain any of this to anyone, even to myself, is that it is impossible to imagine. We always imagine other worlds by imagining this one."

"We put wings on a horse!" Olin exclaimed.

"Yes. Pegasus. Monsters. Faeries. They are the other-worldly-this-world; it doesn't help me in my work. It is, I think, I sort of fear, my *imagination* that is the problem. I'm trying to think about another world, another universe. I do the math and the math points at the possibility. But when I describe it to myself, when I write about it in my notes, I reconfigure only what I already know, have seen already, or felt. There's only this world to imagine another. It is a serious problem for me. The world becomes what I imagine of a world."

"It doesn't sound like science," I said.

"It isn't science, Daniel. It's Proust," Olin offered, "who writes not only of himself, and the endless parties, and the social hierarchies, but also of the multiple selves inside the self, one self a stranger to the other, the other self this self imagines, and the odd times when two versions of the self, like two books open face to face, occupy the same instant of time, and how the world bends its relation to time so that time is ambivalent, moves in two directions, past and future, and more directions than that, and Albertine, dead Albertine, sends a telegram to our narrator who, knowing she is dead, reads the note and believes she is alive. He misread the name; that's what he did—he didn't read it right, he made a mistake." Olin took a sip of wine. "Literature and physics, the muses holding hands."

"Do you teach Proust?" Lydia asked.

"Oh, I do. That's all I teach. I just refuse to do it in a class. I simply make the moment Proustian when I can, without anyone taking note of the lesson. I rescue Proust from his pages and put him back into the world. It's people knowing they're being 'taught' that makes education impossible. The mind loves to get in the way of itself, and then we think we are thinking."

"You're jaded, Olin," I said.

"I know. And so are you. But you, unlike me, are, as you'd say, an *Isolato*."

Lydia raised her eyebrows. "An *Isolato*?"

"Our friend Daniel is a Melvillian; he seems sane, but trust me, underneath the calm exterior is a man capable of feeling the cold November of his soul in any month, and is equally capable of shipping out to the tropics. Save for him, November is the endless month in which every class occurs, and to ship out he must build his own boat—the novel he talks about writing, but hasn't."

I felt a degree of chagrin, Olin revealing more about me than I would have revealed about myself; I was glad of it. He painted a picture of me for Lydia—and did this, I suspect, on my behalf—that gave me a darker substance, a greater mystery, than I could paint for myself. Olin, our little Marcel, was trying to make me an object of romance.

"Melville named—well, Ishmael named—the men on the whale ship *isolatos* . . . each man an island to himself."

"A sad vision."

I looked at Lydia. "It is—" The moth had ceased flying; it walked the top of the lampshade's circle. Olin stared at it as we talked. "—a vision that changes."

"Death is such a nuisance," Olin said in a low voice, talking it seemed to himself, "always reminding us it's around." He looked up. The atmosphere of the night had inexplicably changed. There was in the air a sorrow we felt and could only dispel by talking not of it, but through it.

"I've not been reading *Moby-Dick*, but *The Encantadas*, a short work on the Galapagos Islands. Those islands, many sailors say, are made of what they call 'clinkers.' The ground wasn't normal ground, but comprised of hard and resonant rocks that, stepped on, dully ring like a muffled bell. Sailors when they landed there would scratch their names on these rocks. And sailors yet to come would arrive and step on those names when they stepped on the rocks, and the name wouldn't be spoken, but would ring out."

"It's a beautiful image," Lydia said. "Is it true?"

"I don't know. I only read books; I don't actually *live*. I've only read about those islands. I've never been, though my father has."

"And did he step on the names and make them ring?"

"I don't know. He didn't mention it. Though I imagine it that way." I paused, hesitant at the night's unexpected intimacy. "That feels to me to be what a novel is, stepping on the ground and every step rings out a name—it's what I would like to write, but can't seem to start." I felt I needed to change the tone of what I was saying, self-pitying and self-defeating as it was becoming. "I like this thought of stepping on the names to learn them, reading as an act of the body more than the mind. Reading might be a vast ruse. We are distracted by the names because we understand them—the names for everything. But our mind is more the stick that strikes the gong than we can admit. We don't often hear the music beneath the speaking, the chime beneath the names."

Lydia looked off into the room as if searching for her thought. "There is," Lydia said, "a drone at the edge of the universe that marks the moment of its creation, a constant hiss, not music, but the sound against which music could be heard. It sounds like breath leaking through tightly pressed lips. No, like a mother hushing a child to sleep. I've listened to it. It surrounds everything. It marks the edge, astronomers like to say, of what's known."

"Like the mouth that holds the shape of the last word said," though why I responded with these words, I don't know.

The moth flew from the lampshade and landed on one of the half-melted candles, and Olin, either in anger or disgust, tried to swat it, knocking it over. The flame went out as it fell, but the wax splattered onto the table, onto my plate, a single drop suspended on the tines of my fork, cooling as I watched.

I walked home that night knowing I would fall in love with Lydia. I went home along the walkway, each slab of cement a clinker that said over and over again the names of those I love, *mother father sister mother father sister,* and in that repeating phrase, another name added to the music, hers, *Lydia.* In another universe I wasn't so sad. Somewhere, the laws were different. Gravity wasn't a grave. Somewhere my mother and sister lived; somewhere my father lived with us, singing his song, his translated song, his song whose music re-created the world. Somewhere he was singing it, singing inside it, living inside the song he sings, as all of us do, together.

I went home that night and sat at my desk. I took out one piece of paper from the old ream my father kept in the bottom drawer, the same paper on which he scribbled the notes for his translation, the musical paper, and in the lines of the first staff, I wrote: *I learned to be a quiet child.*

✷

The breeze blew the lilac's scent away from me; I was no longer within it; and with the fragrance, the memory left too. My book bag heavy in my hand. I was—as usual—late for class.

CHAPTER 5

THE PEARL FELL THROUGH THE WATER.

Pearl lay on her bed, awake but dreaming. Mother had said she could not leave her room, would have no dinner, would put herself to bed.

It was the vernal equinox, though Pearl did not know this. The day was divided exactly in half: half light and half dark. She lay on the blue square of her bed, on top of the covers, watching the light change; her thoughts were below the sea. The pearl was falling through the water.

The white whale watched as it fell in front of its eye. And Pearl saw so many things, so many more things than the pearl that had fallen through the grating into the ocean underneath the house. A picture in a frame fell through the water as an oak leaf falls off a tree, shuttling gently back and forth as it descends, a picture of a woman holding a blue umbrella, pink cheeks, looking gently down so that her eyes could not be seen; a woman who looks like her mother. Pearl remembered her mother's blue umbrella, remembered her mother opening it over her head when the rain started to fall, and how it looked to Pearl as if her mother were opening a clear blue sky underneath the dark one, a sky in which no storm could occur. And there it was!—the blue umbrella open, open in the water, falling so much slower than the pearl and the picture. Bubbles rose while objects fell; little circles of breath that no one breathed, or who breathed them?—she did not know. The white whale swam among them all, a cord tangled around its giant body. An apple tree in blossom. How did it fall in the ocean?

Pearl stared at the ceiling, now gently lighter than the dark-filling room. She stared up into the blank wall and saw the tree falling through the water, so peaceful a motion, each blossom attached, nothing lost, swaying as the current moved through it as it would have moved in the wind; it looked like a wedding dress falling through the air. Pearl watched the white whale open its mouth. It was larger than her bedroom; it was, she thought, the size of her house. A little girl could live her whole life in a mouth like that, making a bed in the papery billows, breathing the air it breathed, the room lit by a candle in its head, burning on the whale's own oil. She would be inside it as it swam among all the lost objects. She would sleep when it slept, whose only bed is the ocean's bed, scratching words in its skin as it rolls in its dreams around. She could see it. The white whale opening its mouth.

It was then that Pearl understood what she must do. She thought she could hear her mother crying in her bedroom; but her mother wasn't crying. Pearl knew she must retrieve what she lost and give it back to her mother. She must dive into the ocean, the ocean under the bed.

She crawled under the bed, lifted the grating off the duct. It was a much larger hole than she thought it would be.

Pearl fell into the water.

CHAPTER 6

"DANIEL, YOU'RE QUITE LATE FOR YOUR OFFICE HOURS. They are written *quite* plainly on this card." The chair leaned closer to the card tacked onto my door, as if to see it in a new regard that might mitigate or regird his ire. "Wednesday, 9:30 a.m." Looking down at his watch. "And it's almost 10:00."

"You're right. I apologize. I'm not in the habit of being late. I somewhat lost track of time this morning." He nodded once, curtly, almost martially, and started to turn around. Slightly under my breath, realizing I shouldn't say it even as I did, "Students never come to office hours anyway."

"And why, Daniel, do you think that is?" He pivoted on one foot a half circle to face me again, his wiry eyebrows raised above his eyeglasses like two crescent moons, covered in moss or dust, over the planetary sheen of his eyeglass lenses.

"Students have changed. They are, well—disgustingly self-sufficient."

"No, Daniel, you have changed." He waited for my reaction, an atmosphere of tension he conjured in the hallway to see if I would cry or confess or storm away in insult and anger. I stood there, book bag in hand, and, sighing, leaned against the doorframe. An instructor hurried by, looking down at the ground, her heels' knocking echoing behind her.

"How have I changed?"

"Have you read your evaluations lately?" A dumb-founded stare. "Well, have you?"

"No, I haven't."

"What used to be glowing praise about your enthusiasm, your love, your infectious way of convincing students to care about what they read, of getting them to think, have all changed their tenor to concerns about your disinterest, your apparent boredom, and so on. You used to inspire, and now you," looking flustered, stammering, "you—you *expire*. You, you—read from notes." His attempt to upset me had only upset himself. He looked on the verge of tears. He started to lift one hand to put it on my shoulder, and then, thinking better of it, put it in the pocket of his jacket, and continued down the hallway, farther away from his own office, shaking his head as he went.

"Thank you for bringing this to my attention," I called out down the hall after him. And without turning around, he took his hand from his pocket and waved the back of it at me three times before plunging it again out of sight.

I went into my office and closed the door. My desk I kept perfectly clear. Books on the shelves in alphabetic order. No photos on the walls; only a clock whose minute hand vibrated when it clicked into place. A

window overlooked the green where students hurried
between classes, where the old oak with the obtuse burl
grew more grotesque by the decade. A dead fly on the
windowsill; I picked it up carefully by the tip of one
wing; its forelegs pressed together as if in anticipation or
prayer; I dropped it in the wastepaper basket. *As if I
needed a reminder,* I thought. To inspire one must be
inspired. I had been and now . . . it was, or I was, or both
were, changed. Not that the books I taught had fallen in
my love or regard for them. The opposite. I loved them
as much as I ever had, maybe more; I just felt incapable
of being loved by them in return. Somehow I had made
myself unworthy of the words, those others' words—
words that had put in my mind worlds, a careful disorder I lived within and out from which I looked at my
students and invited them in. The classroom is its own
peculiar cosmos, built not of natural laws, but of laws of
attention—sympathetic chords that the teacher plucks in
himself so as to secretly force the same note to vibrate in
his student. How does one learn?—that is an awful,
unanswerable question. I wanted my students to suffer a
confusion that clarified, to leave the classroom unable to
explain even to themselves what had just occurred over
the previous two hours, as if, once one stepped back out
the threshold of the classroom's door the spell had been
broken, one had unwittingly drunk from the river Lethe
by stepping over it, invisible though it may be, and the
distinct memory of the discussion, what the discussion
brought light to, slowly disappeared in content even as it

remained in form, an empty form whose emptiness was the only reminder that it had once been full, world-full, thought-full, but a few minutes ago. Knowledge was this absence of knowing—*that* is what I taught, thought. But how could I have suspected I would become my own philosophy? That from within emptiness I would have only emptiness to offer? To speak about pages as if they were still blank, to hold them up and say, *See, do you see—say it if you do—that underneath these words the page is blank? The words disguise that blankness as meaning in order to secretly imbed the blankness in you. Words speak around a silent heart. A word is a giant who buries his heart in silence where it can never be found, and in the silence it pulses, not a sound, but sound's opposite, a blank deafness of muteness inside a simpler quiet, the mind's quiet when it seems to say to itself, I'm ready to think, and then waits for thought to begin.* Blank faces, they all look at you, little planets above the flat plane of their desks. It isn't a look of expectation, not of hope, not of yearning—it is a look of fact, the fact of itself. The eye is a dark tunnel behind which mysterious processes occur—distraction and judgment. Behind the eye is the clear pool Narcissus stares into and drowns; but so too is Echo's echo chamber, all the words others speak to us rebounding against the skull only to be spoken back. The world is the condition of asking others to love you by using their own words to convince them to do so. Infinite repeat. Day after day of walking from my office, walking down the hall, down the stairs, to the classroom where students were still assembling, the dark wainscoting adhering to the wall, waiting for them to sit, for chatter to subside, not a silence of patience, but the old chaos in whose silence alone meaning could occur; saying over and over again, countless times, *let's open our books, let's open our books,* the sound of the pages being thumbed through, *let's open our books,* specifying a page, a specific word, the breath in a sentence one comma requires you to take, *let's open our books.* It is a form of enchantment. Professor as conjure-man, professor as initiate, professor as medicine man, professor as holy fool, shaking the book as a shaman shakes the rattle, beating the book as the shaman beats the drum—but it ends. It does not end well. The hand drops from its power, or the power drops from it the hand.

I try to not let myself feel how it is I feel.

I try not to remember; I write so I don't need to remember—let the pages live that life.

But I fail.

The dead fly I'd thrown in the trash bin rattled weakly against the metal, not dead at all. The metal amplified the sound, a buzzing that didn't fill the room but annoyed the ear, the flightless wings trying to fly. I don't know why, I don't know why it must be so, all of it—that it is as it is, has been as it has been, my life; my life's transparent wing. I looked out the window at the oak, blue storm-light darkening the sky, and I thought, *I can't bear it.*

No, I said it to myself differently. I said, *It can't be borne.*

I left my office, locking the door behind me. I told the secretary that I felt ill, and needed to cancel class; would she please be so kind as to tape a note to the classroom door? Thank you. I left Trillbyrne Hall and walked across the green, across the campus to the old chapel to the north, the chapel with the cemetery behind it, the headstones of old professors, some so old the marble lettering's sharp cuts had eroded away into faint impressions, names returning to nothing. My father's headstone was among them. So was my mother's. So was my baby sister's. My whole family in the ground behind the chapel where the devotional bells marked the hours, and the stones mutely absorbed them, counting time a lesser fact than time's end. All the ringing stops.

I didn't kneel down. I didn't break into tears. No memories flooded my mind. I read the stones—*father, wife, child* (with a lamb on the stone's curved top)—over and over again until the words ceased to be words, ceased to give a name to that which has no name, to those who have no names, ceased to insist that it can be spoken of, the world, and the people in it, those we love, who gave us life and for whom we lived. I know what it is: a stone in orbit. The sun is a golden bell. I could see it up there, behind the clouds, a perfect circle. A perfect circle—

"Father," I said, "remember the apple tree."

CHAPTER 7

I WENT HOME. MY MOTHER WAS HANGING ON THE WALL; I looked at her and in my strange distraction the image turned a corner in my mind's labyrinth, and for a moment a thought of the Furies put the Furies in my eye, sitting on a grassy knoll catching their breath; and then I looked away. I went into the study and pulled out the novel again—the hundreds of pages held together by rubber bands, the first pages written on my father's musical sheets, then a thick cream watermarked vellum, then thin newsprint and more gray, and so on, as if the book's progress could be measured in geological strata, sedimentary layer upon layer, pressure pushing the book into form. The first pages weighed heavy on the last, a fossilizing pressure. Written by hand, over the scales of the musical staff so that the lines cut through the letters, the title: *An Impenetrable Screen of Purest Sky*. I read the last sentence written, *It was my sister*—words written just that morning, but which felt an age ago. I have no memory of her. I picture a baby with her mouth open, but I'm only imagining it. Or I see her milky-blue eyes looking up as if into the other world from which she was just pulled and back to which she must soon return—the look of nostalgia. But I'm making it up. Father wandered through the halls holding her as she

68

died, as his wife lay dead in their bedroom, but he never bent down to let me see her. I heard her breathe, and I heard her cry; I heard when breathing and crying ended. I turned the page back over. Blank. I looked at the thick volume of all those handwritten pages, of all those thousands of words, each one of them containing a little breath. I thought the pages held their breath, that this was the meaning of a book—that it was holding its breath for as long as it could. It was afraid it might drown. I pushed the breath aside on the desk, and pulled from a drawer a sheaf of letters I've read and reread, read and reread, for what feels like my whole life. My whole life spent holding my breath—

Call me Daniel. I have a gift I keep to myself, the gift of self-abandon. It is the orphan's lesson if he can learn it— not to feel abandoned, but to continue his abandonment past the bounds of where the loss should end, parent's death that prefigures one's own. Fate is everywhere speaking; it does not call you by name; it tells you to name yourself. Call me Daniel. It is the name my father called me, and it is the name I call myself. It is as real as any name; it works just as well. Call it out to me as I walk down the street and I will turn around, smile or wave, perhaps even walk over to you to chat or reminisce. I have trained myself to do exactly this, as I know you've also trained yourself. "Daniel"—and I turn around and say *yes* quizzically but warmly; I look up and recognize you because you recognized me, whoever it is you are, who knows what it is you know of me. The Furies pursue names through the desert places, the guilt on the names, repeating the names between each other, *Daniel, Daniel, Allan, Allan* to incite each other to volcanic anger, spitting the names out ahead of themselves to run all the faster, *Allan, Allan,* pursuing the guilty names. A writer (I've learned to make no mistake about it) is a lesser Fury—writing down the names while a moth climbs back up the leg of the chair it fell from—not accusing someone else of his guilt, of her misdeeds, but participating in the guilt, recreating it so as to relive it, to share it, not to judge it; the only accusation says in its fated tongue *you were there without me,* but now I am there with you, faulty and necessary witness, fictional but true, here I am with you, Father, Father, call me—

Dear Daniel,

I am in my stateroom on the only boat that would take me as a passenger. If I didn't have money to offer, where would I be? The captain doesn't trust me, nor do the men.

I won't say sorry because I know you understand. I know you will understand. These letters will help you understand.

It is hard to write on the desk as the boat rocks on the waves. I hope you'll be able to read all the words. I've discovered many new aspects of the scroll since your mother died. Her death has helped me as a translator. I hope that doesn't sound callous to you. It made me understand something about this language I could not understand before. Maria, her name, when she was alive, I could speak it and she would come. Now I can say Maria *and mean her exactly, but because she cannot hear me, she cannot come. The same word still calls out, even into death—*Maria. *This is one of the scroll's lessons. Living makes us think that every word ends at the thing it names, but it isn't true. Things live in the middle of their names to distract us from all a word says that is not discernible. We've learned to stop at what is at hand and be satisfied, a child asking for a bauble. But death removes from us what we love, and then the word pushes out past its normal limit, drops its reference from itself, and its sense turns into a singing in which a word ceases to mean any one thing, a singing that opens up abstraction, the interstitial connection between forms—the way an apple seed is also the apple tree is also the apple blossom is also the apple fruit, but more, the way it is also the pollinating wind, also the bees, also the child that, plucking a fruit from the branch, bites into it.* "Apple" *is a word in the myth. I've spent the morning translating it. It cannot be written down, for writing stills it— a kind of death. It must be held in the mind in all its singing complexity. Then the word contains in it all its history, every utterance is in each utterance, a line that stretches back to the first time it was spoken. The word is a realm that includes us all. The mythic word, the ur-word, spoken unknowingly by the fruit vendor on the street, by mothers and daughters, it reaches back to that first saying, when to name something was to create it. A dictionary—no one teaches us this—is a book of ontology. But a spoken word springs forward, too. To say* apple *predicts the countless times the word will be said again, forges the connections that do not yet exist, a man not yet born giving an apple to the woman he loves but she also does not yet exist; to* *say* apple *includes them. A word—and this is why your mother's death has opened me to my work—has nothing to do with time. We infect our language with our own mortality. But the word is outside of time, and refuses to do time's work. Some poets know this. "But you shall shine more bright in these contents / Than unswept stone, besmeared with sluttish time." A word is a small thing in the world, Daniel, but it contains the world. To learn how to speak is to learn how to be in the world—not in the day, but the world past the limits of the day, the old world that doesn't exist in time, the world in which nothing has been lost, the heroic world of monsters and gods. The singer's world.*

The myth on the scroll, it is a song of that unending, that never-yet-begun, world. To sing it opens it up. The mouth is a kind of door, or maybe the entrance to a cave. Plato's cave— where in the mind a word throws a shadow on the wall. To sing the words turns us around, and we step out of our own mouths into the real world, and the words that tricked us into seeing a world that didn't exist are the same words we use to describe the world that does.

I had to leave. I'm not sorry.

I'm sorry that you are too young to understand this letter. One day you will understand. One day I'll teach you this song and then the song will be yours.
Love,

My father left and Grandma Clarel moved in, drinking instant coffee in the living room. She wouldn't talk about him, save to refer in vague terms to "his trip." Letters

72

would arrive almost every week. *A letter, Daniel, a letter,* and in her exasperation she would fan herself with the envelope that she meant to give to me, looking aghast as I kept reaching up toward her face to grab it, saying *stop it, stop it,* and then seeing the letter in her own hand, give it to me, and, bright red, flustered, return to the kitchen. I'd go to my father's study, sit under his desk, and read them over and over again. I didn't understand them, but his handwriting was so distinctly his, the page in my hands seemed like a kind of embrace. I read them so often I memorized them—no, not memorized them. It was not memory. The letters imbued themselves in me. I couldn't quote a single sentence from them; I saw the world through their pages. I would look up, once the letter had been read, at the bookshelf. There, in green with gilt lettering, sat *Wonders and Tales.* It was a book I never read from again, even as, in my child's mind, it kept calling to me to retrieve it, calling me to it—

Dear Daniel,

I must tell you about the myth, but it is hard to do. To write it down too precisely betrays it. But you should know it, the parts of it you can know.

Beneath the sky another sky opened;
within the sea another sea.
In this sea one creature lived:
a white whale. It swam through the sea.
There was no land; there was only water. The whale was no god, but without the whale no god could exist. Time did not

divide day and night; there was no day and night. The whale was like an island, but there was no land.

A flame inside the whale's head spoke to it; the voice said "dive down." The white whale dove to the sea's bed, swam among the ragged rocks that cut the whale's skin, carved into its skin words the flame inside its head chanted as it swam among the cutting rocks. The whale's whole body was etched with words when the voice in the flame said "leave," and then the whale left. It did not take a breath. The white whale swam to a desert place where the sea-bed's soft sift lay deep and undisturbed by a single mark. The voice said "sleep" and the whale slept, and in its sleep it rolled in the sand, pressing into the seabed the words carved on its skin. It rolled in its sleep until every word carved into its skin was pressed into the sand it slept on. And in its sleep it dreamed.

The whale dreamed a dream of the sun over the land, a sun it had never seen; it dreamed the sun when it slept on the word sun pressed into the sand. The sun cast its warmth on the ground and from the ground a seed sprouted, and in the whale's dream the seed became a tree full of white blossoms, and from the blossoms blew the seeds of other plants, of every plant, seeds the sun warmed until they sprouted, and then the land was green; the whale dreamed of this tree when it slept on the word apple pressed into the sand. There were no animals and no people in the dream. When the whale awoke the voice in the flame said "breathe" and the whale swam up to breathe, and there it saw the sun and the green land. The whale took a breath and the voice in the flame said "dive down" and the whale dove down, dove faster when the voice said "faster." The *white whale dove at great speed and when the voice in the flame said "die" the whale struck the seabed with its head, struck the seabed with such force its head cracked open and the sperm escaped into the ocean, each drop becoming an animal as it rose, every animal as it all rose, fish and turtles swimming in the water, birds springing into the air, deer and antelope, lions and elephants, stepping onto shore, and humans, crawling from the water and standing up walking toward the fruit hanging from the apple tree. The whale when it died opened a chasm at the bottom of the ocean, the bottom of the world. The whale's broken body fell into the chasm.*

There were two of every living thing. The man and the woman lived in the green world, eating from the tree, and another person lived inside the woman. She knew another person lived inside her, but could not tell the man; there were no words to speak, and nothing could be known. So the woman left the man and he watched her leave; she walked to the shore and walked into the sea and sunk down to the seabed where she read the words printed in the sand.

When the woman read the word "breathe" she tried to take a breath but could not; the air was far above her. She tried to swim up to the air but she could not, and when she could swim no more, she fell into the chasm where the white whale had fallen.

She fell into the whale's open mouth; and the baby was inside her.

There is more, Daniel—but enough—this is the story you should know—
Love,

75

Father's letters grew less frequent but more wild. He wrote to me as if he were telling himself secrets—

Dear Daniel,

*You are another me and that makes everything harder and eas-
ier. The men here won't talk to me. They go about their work,
and it's through their work they know the world. They each own
a "sea eye." They read the ocean's surface and they read the
clouds on the horizon. I eat at night with the captain, who smiles
cordially as he pours me some wine but he eyes me suspiciously.
I have no sea eye. A deckhand found me last night on the prow
in a gale wind chanting into the storm, chanting the myth. He
turned me around but I was as if in a trance and I didn't see him
but kept on in my song and so he left me there in the danger
hoping I'd blow away. I know of it only because I hear the whispers. There are no secrets on a ship—everything will out.*

*There are words for the wind that can calm it, and there are
words to force it to such violence it breaks a bird in flight in
half—not* words, *one word said differently in the song.*

It's dangerous to speak.

*Underneath the words on the scroll are a series of lines I've
never understood. They don't modify the words above them, nor
is the line consistent—thicker in places, thinner in others, as is
a calligraphic line. It is written in a different ink, I think by a
different hand—as if, as if the old Jesuit's helper had brought
the scroll to someone, shaman or wise man or healer or singer,
and that man added in these lines to correct or finish the scribe's
work. But last night in the gale I understood. Singing into the
wind the gale spoke underneath my words, a drone against*

76

which the myth's song could be heard. The song is double-voiced, can only be sung truly by two people. One must sing the unvarying drone, the ground against which the song itself with its words creates what it creates, opens what it opens. A song cannot be sung against absolute silence, a different kind of silence must be created, a silence that isn't silence, a nothing that is instead of a nothing that is not.

I left, Daniel—and I'm sorry for it—but I left because I need help with some difficult points in the song, places where it seems a word must be sung twice in the same instant, sung in such a way where a word means itself and its opposite at once, as light in the song also means darkness, as the word for sun also includes the light of the moon.

So I am sailing to the island, the old island, center of the world.

There is one singer left, Daniel—only one person alive who can sing this song. He came to me in a dream and told me he was dying. Such people can do such things. In my dream he said he has heard me singing this song. He told me he must teach me what is unwritten in the words. He called to me in a dream, and because of this dream I left you. He told me he was dying. He told me time is short. He showed me a map. A tiny island in or near the Galapagos, those islands sailors for centuries would stop at to carry a tortoise away for dinner. Those islands where, when a sailor died while carrying a tortoise, died from heat or exhaustion or sickness, he was lucky enough to be buried on land so he still has a body to be mourned.

I also sound crazy to myself, when I am someone named Allan listening to myself—but I'm not Allan anymore. Not

only. I'm someone anonymous. A singer. A singer is no one and then being no one becomes a kind of everyone. I'm a better father anonymous than I am with a name—
Love,

Father never spoke to me when I was a child as he spoke to me in his letters. When I would stand in the doorway of the study while he worked he looked at me as if I were only a child—the child that I was—and too young to be initiated into his thoughts. He would look up at me with a kind of pity. In the letters his voice was different. He knew they wouldn't only be read by the young boy I then was, but also by the adolescent I wasn't yet, and the young man, and the adult, and sad middle-aged me sitting in the night sheen trying not to cry.

Grandma Clarel would read the letters, too. She knew where I kept them in my room. I didn't hide them, nor did I mind. I wanted company inside their strangeness. She read them sitting on the edge of my bed; I would find her when I came home from school, dabbing a wadded-up tissue to her eye, sniffling loudly, and saying to herself *oh no, oh my* in rapid succession, and when she saw me, she would say *Daniel, you're home, you're home, so early too! Coffee, coffee, it's time for coffee and a snack,* as if singing a song to a tune ever present in her head, and, stuffing the tissue up the end of her sleeve, would smile broadly as if to hide from me her worry, as if I hadn't seen her crying, as if I couldn't see her eyes, her slightly disheveled hair whose strands escaped the bun she kept it in, and seeing that I saw the letter in her hand, would look at me and say *oh this, I was neatening up and it fell to the ground. Come, come with me*—pausing briefly—*Your father is having quite a trip, isn't he?*—

Dear Daniel,
The woman in the chasm in the whale's broken mouth—she is not alive but she is not dead. She is waiting with her child inside her. There are other stories you'll learn. Orpheus descended into the underworld to rescue his beloved Eurydice. He sang a song the darkness itself loved and it parted veillike in front of him. Eurydice followed him, would follow him as long as he sang, as long as his fingers struck the notes, as long as he didn't look back to see if she was following. But he did look back and she was swallowed back into the night, the night that isn't the opposite of day, the other night.
    I'm scared I will look back too—when the time comes—
Love,

The letters grew shorter. He stopped writing our last name on the envelopes; they simply said—

Son, my Son,
    Do you know how much of the world is real? All of it is.
    It is dangerous to speak and it is dangerous not to speak.
    Beneath the song other songs exist;
    beneath the myth other myths.
    The chasm-world is open.
    Songs are doors. Singers betray thresholds.

79

Death is a chasm under life. The song sings it open.
Dark ink on white page.
Opposites embrace when they collide.
The song is a form of life that does not deny death.
Dreams do not teach us to sing but show us there is a song.
The song is a form of death that does not deny life.
Every singer is also sung.
Love,

Father's last letter regained a clarity I thought wholly abandoned—at least, it began so—

Dear Son,
The ship will leave me on the island tomorrow. It will sail away and leave me here. You might receive no letters from me for some time, and I want you not to worry. I will be with the old singer, learning. And when I've learned—

(and here his handwriting changed, lost the canny precision of his cursive hand, closed letters remaining open, a lower case *e* whose line never crossed fully into its semicircle, an *o* incomplete)

                     I will arrive in
your dream and tell you—and I won't be alone—
Love,

CHAPTER 8

I PUT THE LETTERS AWAY AND WENT TO BED. OLD WATER in the water glass on the bedside table. I could taste time in the water when I drank it, stale metal in my mouth. I left the window open even though the spring night was cold. The house empty save for me, would the night breeze increase its absence? *Lydia* was a name I said to myself in the silence of my head. Stale metal in the head.

✷

father sits in my bed reading
the book I am reading
is the book I am writing mysteriously bound

it's about me he says

his eyes are pale he says come with me

father walks outside the house and out
across the lawn he peers in at the window

the study has a lamp lit on the desk

the moth thinks it is a moon
he says the study is mine it's about me

he says follow me his feet remove the dew
from the grass from every blade of grass
the dew wets the cement under his feet as he walks

I walk behind him
he isn't singing but there is a song

in the apple tree in blossom on the rise
my father points at himself he is sitting
in the midst of the blossoms singing all alone

and when he sees me my father
stops his song and says

both of them say my fathers both say

I looked back and I failed

❋

I woke before the alarm and heard the alarm click
before the radio's voice began speaking. Investigators
believe the poet fell off a cliff on the backside of the volcano. They cannot find his body. Investigators report
they found the poet's footprints near the crater of the
volcano. They think he had injured his leg; that he had

weakened. At the cliff's edge the footprints disappear. No one could survive the fall. Further search has been canceled. I clicked the radio off and in the half darkness went to the study. I pulled out the novel and put it on the desk. I picked it up again. Its heft is some form of life that is also my own. The night's dream indelible in my mind.

I looked back and I failed.

Page's poor memory whose poverty is its perfection.

I stood up, novel in hand, and dropped it in the trash bin. It landed with a metallic thud, a single drumbeat, and then all was silent.

I walked out of the office. I walked out of the house. I walked through the dew-wet grass to the window. I stared in at the study, at the desk, where every morning for many years I sat and wrote. I stared into the room at my absence. I was the one who was missing.

CHAPTER 9

IT RANG YEARS AGO—THE PHONE THAT WOKE ME. I'D gone to bed early, strangely exhausted. It was Lydia. "Did I wake you?" I tried to brighten my voice, but sleep was there, occupying it. Lydia's voice in my ear, but her body far away. "I read your novel. I wanted to call and tell you." Her voice spoke outside of time, articulate air.

"Thank you."

"I did wake you. I'm sorry. I just wanted to thank you—"

I spoke thickly through sleep's fog, a kind of amnesiac veil through which I could almost remember myself and almost remember Lydia, a fog wakefulness burned steadily but not quickly away, so that every word I spoke came from a person different than myself, more intimate because more strange, as if I hadn't yet had time to fully assemble myself, and the words leaked out of the gaps as the rosebush peeks through the fog's tatters as morning's heat gathers. "No, I'm awake. I was just thinking about the night."

"Thinking about the night?"

"Thinking in the night, I mean."

Lydia laughed. "Well, I'm sorry to end your thoughts."

"Don't be. Thinking was getting me nowhere. I was thinking the moon was an eye that blinks. It takes twenty-eight days for the eye to blink. The full moon is when everything is seen. The stars are the shapes the moon thinks."

"It sounds like something from your novel."

"I know. Everything does—it's a bit of a problem. The novel is just one long dream that doesn't know it's a dream. But that's only the first part. I think it will be long, long and sprawling and disorderly, tying time in a knot."

"A Gordian knot?"

"A wedding knot."

"The marriage of time? Whom does time marry?"

"Time marries Timelessness. It's a marriage on the rocks."

"I did wake you up, didn't I?"

"Yes, I'm glad you did. Dreaming about the moon gives me headaches. Why don't you come over?"

"Are you sure? It's almost going to be late."

"The warm milk cocktail has worn off, and my eight p.m. nap has rejuvenated me."

"O.K. I will." Lydia hung up the phone, decisive.

I kissed Lydia at the door, her slight blush in the porch-light. I had never kissed her before, not held her or her hand any of the times we had met for coffee or dinner after meeting at Olin's. The crickets chirped. The firefly's luminescent green flash in zigzag behind her and a heartbeat later a green flash in the lengthening grass. The moon squinted down, the only witness. Clouds, a cautious curtain, began to close. The night filled with a privacy that included us. The crickets sang a song that marked a boundary we were inside of; it was about us. I kissed her once more, on the cheek. "Please, come in."

Lydia stepped into the hallway. "Is that your mother in this picture?"

"It is."

Lydia reached into her purse and pulled out the manuscript I'd given her, thirty pages pinched together by a paperclip bent slightly out of shape. The first pages written on my father's sheets for musical notation; in the dim light I could make out the title written in red. Lydia held the pages up so that they spread out like a bouquet, gently rolling her wrist back and forth as she looked longer at my mother's photograph, so that the pages, like a peacock's tail folding and unfolding, kept fanning from side to side, not the blue eyespots of the peacock's feather when fully open, but her eyes, dark brown eyes, now looking at me as the pages' thin lines crossed them. "It's just as you describe," she said, handing me the pages.

"You're the first person I've shown it to," I said as we walked through the hall to the living room, a small fire in the fireplace.

"You haven't shown it to Olin?"

"No. He has a remarkable disdain for contemporary fiction. He thinks death is the first qualification for being able to write. He thinks it's only good taste to give up life before picking up the pen. Mostly, I agree. But here I am, tawdry in the work."

"I don't know if I should ask this, but—is it true?" She sat down.

"Yes." I paused. "No."

Lydia looked at me. "Are you sure you're awake?"

"Yes and no. It's hard to tell."

"Did your father translate a myth?"

"He tried. I don't think he felt that he ever managed it fully."

"Did your mother die? And your sister, too?

"Yes. That's true."

"You're writing an autobiography?"

"I don't think so. I'm not sure, to tell you the truth."

I brushed my hand against her wrist. "It's a novel, I think, about the fiction of the self."

She looked at me as if disappointed that I could say such a thing. "Is the self a fiction?"

"It seems to become one." I pointed vaguely at the pages on the small table separating both our chairs. "I began to write it after our dinner at Olin's. What you said—about worlds next to worlds, worlds within worlds—it reminded me of my father. It sounded like something he would say, or would have said." It almost sounded like nothing at all, just a vibration in the night, the thunder, so far away.

"Is a planet not yet found a fiction?" Lydia seemed flustered or frustrated. She kept clicking the nail of her thumb against the nail of her middle finger, a pensive, half-angry sound. "Is a galaxy past our vision a fiction? A black hole? Dark matter?"

"I'm not sure," I said, taken somewhat aback.

"A theory isn't a fiction. It's a hazardous guess at what's real without the comfort of a fact to say so."

"The self is dark matter?"

"That's not what I'm saying."

"The self is a black hole?"

"No—that's not what I mean; that's not what I mean at all." She looked down at her hands as if they weren't her hands, watching them as she would watch two animals weary in the yard. And then, she turned to me, and picking up the pages I'd written, said "This is the dark matter of the self. Words whose weight holds you together. It's not a fiction if you're really at work on it. It's a theory, an experiment. It will prove you to yourself or nothing will. It's these pages that are the telescope looking inside itself, the contemplation of the mirror where the distant light comes to focus, a question not about *what* is being seen, but a question of *how* it is being seen." She put the pages down. "When I decide I might love someone, when I come over in the night to make love to him, I want him to mean himself when he says *I*. When he tells me he loves me, when he says *I love you,* that can't be a fiction." She stood up. She stood in front of me. She slowly undid the buttons of her shirt. "Do you love me?"

The heaviness in the air before the storm. Lightning-flash lit up a cloud from within itself, a paper lantern.

"I love you." I felt the question in my voice.

Lydia pushed her shirt from off her shoulders and let it fall to the rug.

BOOK THREE

SUMMER

CHAPTER 1

PEARL FELL THROUGH THE WATER.

Pearl let out her breath in little bubbles that rose above her as she watched. She had no end of breath; she did not panic.

The ocean, Pearl thought, is empty but full, like the empty sky that is full with air. She closed her eyes and remembered the air, remembered as she held her breath; she felt no need to breathe. She fell through the water remembering the shadows of cottonwood fluff on the sidewalk, remembered looking up and seeing the seeds floating in the air, so light they didn't seem to fall; she remembered seeing the small shadows of the cotton-wood seeds on the sidewalk darkened by a larger shadow in which the tree disappeared, remembered looking up and seeing clouds. She stood in their shadows and remembered that the clouds took shapes.

A mouse with its front paws pressed together; a fox curved within the curl of its tail; a polar bear scratching its back against a tree; a horse growing wings; an owl hunting; a whale whose tail grew dark as it descended, that grew brilliantly white as it arched back over its body, flukes spreading out. Pearl remembered that when the white whale widened it darkened, too; she remem-bered when it swam overhead. The whale's thoughts rumbled through the world and then the rain began to fall, it shook from its body all the water as it breached over the earth—rain falling in pellets that knocked the cottonwood seeds from the air. Pearl remembered that the whale dove back into itself; it was its own element, its own ocean. It dove into itself and began to disappear: owl folding its wings against its body; horse nestling into the invisible grass; bear hiding its head beneath its paws; fox curling its tail tighter around its body until it becomes the mouse scurrying into itself instead of a hole. Then the sky was calm and blue. The sun dried the ground. The sun a perfect pearl falling across the sky. Pearl remembered seeing the cottonwood seeds in shadow and then looking up to see them floating again in the air.

Pearl's mother wandered through the house, rubbing the hem of her dress between her thumb and finger as she walked. When she sat down she rubbed the cuff of her sleeve; she ran her hand unconsciously along the table's edge; she rubbed her leg against the chair's leg. Everything has an edge, she thought, except what is round. She thought about the lost pearl and then she thought about Pearl, and in her distraction the two thoughts slowly merged: Pearl looking at her from her bedroom and those were pearls that were eyes, the sun on the pearls that were Pearl's eyes, a shadow on the face of the pearl that was Pearl's face, the pearlescent sheen of a ghost and the ghost had Pearl's shape. And when the two thoughts had fully merged, when the lost pearl and her daughter were a single thought, her mother stifled a cry; she felt some space, ocean-wide, ocean-deep, open within her, and she felt as if she were drowning in herself. She could not escape. The moon was above her in the night, a pearl in the starless dark, a single pearl in the night's black box, the night that has an edge it hides from our eyes, the night that is dark so that its edge will not show. But sometimes the moon falls off the edge; when a child pulls it from its box, the moon will sometimes fall off the edge—and as Pearl's mother thought this thought, the moon went out, the moon above the ocean in which she floated went out, not gradually growing smaller, not dimming into nothing, just blinking off, gone.

Pearl's mother stood up from the table and walked to her daughter's room. The door was closed. She opened it. There was the space where her daughter had lain down pressed into the sea-blue quilt.

The room was quiet but not silent. She could hear a rhythmic sound, it filled the room, a sound almost not a sound, a presence, as the ocean unseen in the night is a presence, rolling up on the shore and withdrawing. It sounded as if the ocean were in the room.

Pearl?—no answer.

CHAPTER 2

I SPEND MANY HOURS, AS EVERYONE DOES, LOOKING through glass. There outside the window is the silver poplar in summer's full bloom; this is a fact I know and which you must believe. My house is old and the glass is rippled and fragile. I see the tree; it is there. I'm sorry if this sounds like philosophy. I want to say I know the tree is there, the silver poplar; the wind blows the branches against the pane of the window I see the tree through. I know the tree is there, but I do not believe it. Through the rippled glass it appears to me as, when a boy, I gazed down through the water at the silver minnows, slight waves undulating above the glittering fish, a wave's beveled edge moving the fish when the fish do not themselves move, water catching the sun in scalelike bursts of light that the fish disappear within, though the fish, whose own bodies also catch the light, seem to cause the dazzle of their own absence; I remember reaching my hand through the water and watching them dart away. The branches of the poplar tree are pushed by the wave that is the wind breathing through it, a motion I watch through the old rippled glass. There are mornings when I think I could, as when a young boy by the lakeshore, put my hand through the glass—which is a liquid, after all—and watch it part around my hand. A window is a slow-flowing river, always flowing south, and the glass would part as a river current parts—a small eddy there behind my wrist, and the v-shaped wake formed by the current's speed pointing downriver. But if I did put my hand through, if I could do so, then the poplar would, as the minnows always did, leave in a flash of sunlight on leaf; I won't risk it.

The mind is its own malady. A pane of glass etched on one side by thought and on the other side by the world, and so seldom do the two etchings match that when they do we feel as if the gods have returned, or we feel in the hands of fate or genius or art—or worse, we feel godly, we feel ourselves one of the fates (here are the lines of those threads in my hands), we are the genius, we make the art. By "we" of course I only mean me. The mind is its own malady—fragile, rippled pane.

I spend a lot of time looking out windows; everyone does, I suspect. I wake at dawn as I always do and go to the study, my father's old study, sit at my desk, my father's old desk, and look out the window. There is the silver poplar—which I know exists, it must exist, which I need to exist—gradually, as if from out a fog, appearing distinct from the dark gray light, emerging from the night in whose element it had been, for all I know, fully subsumed; or from the night, in my eye, the tree is daily exhumed. Sometimes I forget the glass is there, that I am seeing through it. Sometimes I forget I am seeing through my eye. Sometimes I look down at the pages in the trash bin, pages I've thrown out but cannot remove; sometimes I notice the way in which the sin-gle pages separate, how from a certain angle the edges appear as palm fronds, and cast upon the page next to them a frond-like knife-edge shadow; sometimes I notice how dark the pages look down at their center when the pages splay outward like the petals from some night-blooming flower—every book being a night-blooming flower the reader enters into headfirst, the pollen smeared inside the ears, dehiscent promise of new dreams unfolding within and replacing the wilting old, desire's buzz a white noise the reader's winged mind no longer hears—or I can see on the faces of disordered pages random words, words now connected in my mind that otherwise would never be joined, a syntax of fate or of chance, *quiet door's already ancient song.* I make note of these sentences, for what it's worth. I think they pin down my straying thoughts as a needle pins down a specimen.

I spend a lot of time—what it is that time is—look-ing out the window in my study. Almost every day there is an hour, and by hour I mean an angle of light, every hour being but an angle of light, in which I see myself looking out the window, looking out at the poplar there in the yard. I see my own reflection. When my mind has wandered too far from me, I see my father in the win-dow looking at me. He has a look on his face I've seen before—the look he often had when he returned from the island. It is a wide-eyed look, as if someone has just asked him a question he had never before asked himself;

and at the same time, a sorrowful look (some forms of surprise also being forms of sorrow), as if in hearing the question, perhaps a question he is only asking himself, he realizes already he has no answer. A helpless look. This look on my face reflected in the glass—there it is again, just now. Why am I always staring through myself to see the world? The poplar tree is a fact, and a fact does not need belief to exist. It would exist without me; I need that to be true. Sometimes I see a face in the window and I realize it's always my face slightly rippled in the rippled glass—a face I can imagine putting my hand through, putting my hand into, if I move my hand slowly enough, grasping in the air or under the water, trying to catch the face before it disappears.

I catch my hand moving in the air as if of its own volition when the phone rings and breaks the magic.

"Hello? Hello?" the voice asked before I could say hello. "Who is this?"

"This is Daniel."

"Daniel?"

"Yes. You called me."

"I know, Daniel. I know that. I just wanted to make sure it was you. You never know if the call does go through to the person you intend it to. It is a troubling and inexact technology. And many people's voices sound alike. It's best to verify. At least, I think so." The chair's voice was nervous and exasperated. "And it is you, which is good, as you are who I wanted to call."

"Is everything all right?" I asked. The chair, in all the years I've taught at the college, all the years he had supervised me in the department, had never called me at home before. I worried he might be calling to renew his concerns about my teaching, or worse, to segue those specific anxieties into more general ones. I worried he might reverse my own question, and archly, voice filled with innuendo, ask me in echo, *Are* you *all right?*, emphasizing *you* with almost cosmic absurdity. I felt annoyed in advance, ready to hang up.

"No, Daniel." He paused, gathering himself. "It's not."

"It's nothing serious, I hope."

"No. Well, yes. I mean, I don't yet know," at which admission he caught his breath, a slight gasp, as if trying to stop himself from crying. "It's Bitsy. I found her this morning fallen over in the kitchen, staring at her bowl of water, and she couldn't get up." Bitsy is the chair's poodle, an ancient dog whose legs for years now trembled as she walked, a creature whose purely timorous nature found her rearing back on her hind legs to turn and flee at the slightest threat—a bird landing in front of her, or a student kneeling down to pet her. The chair kept a photo of her on his desk; she was his only family. He drank coffee from a mug with her portrait transferred in grainy pixels across its surface, an effect I found odd, slightly disturbing, when at faculty meetings I stared at the dog on the mug, her face looked half-hidden behind the veil of her own face, as if she were some ancient Sybil refusing yet to speak her vision.

"I'm sorry. Can I be of help?"

"That's why I'm calling, Daniel. Thank you for asking. I am supposed to teach this afternoon, the last day of my summer seminar. But I need to take Bitsy to the vet—I am distracted. I was hoping you could take my place. The class is on *Moby-Dick,* the end of the book; an hour-long conversation. Then send them off to work on their essays."

Moby-Dick was a class I used to teach every other year; it is a book it would not be unfair to say that I love. I love it to such a degree that it became difficult for me to teach it—not difficult—almost impossible. I would make jokes to my students, *obsessed with a book about obsession,* try to excuse my raving as a natural enthusiasm when more truly I felt caught in the darkness of the work, no, the dark within the darkness of it—it seemed to speak of me as I spoke of it, and at some point, it became too much for me to bear, repeatedly entering into the same pages, my old copy with marginalia in different colors filling the margins, the same thoughts worded differently across the years, always reaching the same conclusion, Ahab and the white whale, yes, but even more so Ishmael, orphan Ishmael, who saved himself by putting his arms around his friend's empty coffin, a coffin engraved with the tattoos that covered his friend's body, so that the coffin was itself his friend, and whose etchings were an entire treatise, a whole epistemology, on the working mystery of the universe. No one can read it.

"I haven't read it in years. I'm sure I wouldn't do a worthwhile job. Have you thought of asking Olin?"

"Daniel, please. It would be a favor to me. I'd look upon your helping me out quite favorably."

I could see that I was trapped. I would have spent my afternoon jotting down abstract notes about the course I was planning for the fall, a course on wonder and wonderment, on enchantment and symbol—a nearly useless activity. "Of course. I'm sorry I hesitated."

"Thank you, Daniel. The class is at two o'clock in the old seminar room."

"I hope Bitsy will be O.K."

On hearing her name he hiccupped. "Yes," he said, his voice strained and high, and then, calming himself, "I hope so too."

After the call had ended, I continued to hold the receiver for some time, staring out the window. It was now fully morning, I thought, as the dial tone began its low, ceaseless buzz. I put the phone in its cradle.

I walked over to the bookshelf and pulled *Moby-Dick* out, sat down with it at the table, set it on its spine, and let it fall open. *Chapter CIII, A Bower in the Arascides.* On the left-hand page, underlined in three different colors of ink, so that the last red line clipped the top of the letters below it, *The weaver-god, he weaves; and by that weaving is he deafened, that he hears no mortal voice; and by that humming, we, too, who look on the loom are deafened; and only when we escape it shall we hear the thousand voices that speak through it.* I closed the book and looked out the window. I heard a robin's startled cry, and then saw it fly up from the grass below my vision. It landed on a thin branch, a branch too thin to hold its weight, and its momentum carried it forward even as its talons clenched the twig, so that the bird spun and hung upside down; it could not right itself; it seemed unwilling to let go and fall to the ground or to fly away as it fell. I could not see what had scared it. I just watched it holding on to the branch— this just a moment. And then it did let go, and fell down to the grass it had fled. I guess that it felt the danger had passed, or that the danger was a danger no longer; it had acquainted itself with its horror—staring at it upside down from the swaying branch—become sociable with it, and returned.

CHAPTER 3

IT WAS THAT SUMMER, THAT REFULGENT SUMMER LONG ago when breathing was its own luxury, that I last read *Moby-Dick*—that summer Lydia and I were in love. We read it together, each separately, but at night reading aloud favorite passages to each other, passages that occasionally would be the same. Ishmael on the masthead, Lydia and I beneath the white sheets. *Let me make a clean breast of it here, and frankly admit that I kept but sorry guard. With the problem of the universe revolving in me, how could I—being left completely to myself at such a thought-engendering altitude—how could I but lightly hold my obligation to observe all whale-ship's standing orders, "Keep your weather eye open, and sing out every time."*

"It's lucky I'm not alone in the heights," I'd say, "what with the problem of the universe sitting here beside me as it whirls around within me."

"It is a problem, isn't it?" And then grabbing the edge of the sheet, and giving it a quick tug upward so that the cloth billowed above our bodies, revealing us to ourselves, she would sing out, "Thar she blows!"

I remember her body then, her white body beneath the sheet's gauzy light—her living body impossible to speak of or define. It was a woman's body, breasts and hips, a pale body, and it was Lydia's. A body with a name.

To say her name the tongue presses against the backside of the front teeth, draws back to the top of the palate, liquid to plosive, and then the tongue drops, the mouth opens as the hard *e* lowers into the long *a,* the tongue just edging over the bottom teeth, and the name is said, it is spoken, expelled with the breath as the sheet falls back down, as she turns toward me, having heard her name . . .

"But you know what the danger is?"

"Of hunting whales? I'd guess it is the whales."

"No, of thinking alone on the masthead."

"Yes? That you fall down."

"Right. But it's what you fall into."

"The ocean."

"Yourself."

She looked at me, the sheet fully settled back over us, under the waves again. "That's why it's good not to be alone."

I hold now in my hand that same book I read that summer with her, carrying it from the study, in between the hallway's white walls that somehow seem to press toward me, glass picture frames only a brilliant white sheen showing nothing of the faces they covered. I walked to the hook where my book bag hangs, opened its flap, and put the novel in. I'd long ago thrown out the notes I kept diligently for many years—my attempt at thinking intricately enough to trace the intricacy of the book, those yellowed pages bound together by a rubber band, my mind outside my mind, words to remember what otherwise I might forget. I put the novel in, spine first so the thumb-dirty pages faced upward, and snapped the bag shut. Taking it from the hook, I walked out the door to school. It felt empty. But in my head the book was heavy, an anchor-weight plunging my mind again to airless depths. The summer day today eerily calm, no wind, no breeze. The waters were still. Or would be still, if I were on the water. The trees looked to my eye burdened by the weight of their leaves, as if the very thing that sustained them, that took in the light that fed them, was their most intimate threat. Invisible within one tree a house finch sang. I walked underneath the song. The broken shell of a robin's egg on the path, smear of yolk, but no tree above it from which it could have fallen.

That refulgent summer long ago, *that* summer, when Lydia and I were in love, we went to the art museum downtown to see the new exhibition. We walked up the granite stairs and through the revolving door in the opaque glass wall that was the museum's front, only to see ourselves approaching ourselves in the mirrored surface of a faceless rabbit standing attentively in the foyer. Actually, we appeared twice. First in the belly, our images growing less distended as we neared the polished curve; then in the rabbit's featureless face, our heads' dark upside-down circles where the rabbit's eyes should have been, as if he was using us in order to see us.

"*Reason and Appetite,*" I said, reading the title on the placard on the wall.

Lydia took me by the hand and guided me through a milling crowd of students to a side room in which the museum displayed objects from its permanent collection, curators selecting objects according to a theme. The word REFLECTION was written in bright metal above the door. Against a sheet hanging in the middle of the room a film loop showed a cupped hand filled with water, and on the water's surface, the face of the man holding it; every second or two small ripples would disrupt the portrait of himself he was holding—his heartbeat—and then his face would appear in his own hand again. A broken mirror on the floor. A pair of mirrored shoes on a pedestal, each on a separate motorized cylinder that, at regular intervals, clicked the heels together. A string dripped water onto a mirror flat beneath it: its surface, perfect elsewhere, is slightly marred by the water dropping onto it; the eye works out the process in reverse, imperfection in the perfect surface, noticing the water drop that out of its own destruction builds an instantaneous crown, to the string from which the water dropped; and looking at the string, seeing a mirror on the wall directly behind it, a mirror that had been through the same process, which had on its surface a dark crater that, when standing before it, water dripping off the string in front of your gaze, put a hole in the middle of your face. A painting of a man looking in a mirror and seeing the back of his own head. And set against an entire wall, a series of different-sized mirrors each in a different frame, some ornate, some austere, one with no frame at all, an oval mirror hanging by a string tied around a nail in the wall.

"It's called *Family Portrait*," Lydia said, reading from the pamphlet accompanying the show. "The artist asked each member of his family, parents, wife, children, to choose a mirror of his or her liking. He placed the mirror on the wall and asked each person to look at herself. He borrowed a machine from the psychology lab at the University that recorded the motion of each person's eye as she looked at herself—the 'saccadic motion' it says here. Then for parents and wife and children he etched those lines—the eye's motion when one looks at oneself—on the mirror each had chosen."

I walked over to a mirror in golden baroque frame, clusters of grapes in gold, sparrows and finches in gold, ivy twining in gold that on closer inspection was a golden paint chipping off from the wood in many places; I could see the grain of the wood on the finch's beak whose wing tip was broken. On the mirror's surface were a bunch of lines, hundreds of lines, a chaos at first that began, on looking closer, to take order if not shape. There was no outline of head or of face. Only lines clustered together, hinting at what was being seen: thick crosshatches marking what must be the mouth, and linking the mouth, in a series of jagged diagonal lines, the right eye, marked by the overarching brow, and with a set of compact circular lines that marked what looked like two pupils in a single eye. And then the eye was my eye, and I was seeing my face through the face of another. I felt suddenly awful. I had put on the mask of another person's eyes. Then Lydia's face was next to my own. She said, "Look," pointing at the small placard next to the mirror, a placard I hadn't noticed, "this is a self-portrait."

"It is?"

"Yes. It's titled *Me.*"

I looked back in the mirror, my face inside his face, my eyes in his eyes.

"So, that's 'Me,'" I said, and walked out of the room by myself, turning around at the door to see Lydia absorbed by the same portrait, and a slight step back of shock when she saw her eye caught in the artist's.

We walked down the hall of old arms and armor, reliquaries and goblets. A shield with a gun's muzzle pointing out its center. Saint's tooth in a glass box.

"There was something awful about that, wasn't there?" Lydia said.

"About those mirrors?"

"Yes." She looked to her side at a rifle whose butt inlaid with ivory depicted a unicorn fleeing hunting dogs and the hunters behind them. "To see yourself as someone else. To be a stranger like that. But more: It's *intimate.*" She said the word as if in awe and disgust. "You stand in front of a mirror every day, and every day it shows you exactly whom you'll know you'll see—just yourself. It's good to know, somehow, isn't it, that you're yourself and no one else?"

"I'm kind of taken by the thought of being someone else," I said, trying to recover my humor, to find a way to remove us from the strangeness of the hour.

But Lydia kept along the lines of her thought, tucking a strand of hair back behind her ear. "We think we're checking our hair, checking to see if anything is stuck in our teeth, if we look presentable—but it's a different question, one we're always asking but never say." She stopped talking, but she wasn't quiet. There was an inward noise in her face. We walked past a gallery in which I saw a woman in a painter's smock, easel in front of her, exactly reproducing on her canvas the painting she was looking at, a lioness with a blood-red mouth drinking from a pool. "The eye doesn't know it, but sight is anonymous." She said this with finality, as if she had reached a scientific certainty.

"What's the riddle?" Exasperated, but trying to hide it. "You're speaking as if you've answered the riddle."

She pointed into a glass case where a face painted on a porcelain platter had cracked in half. "Just that. I don't know how else to say it. It's not just seeing myself through another person's eyes—that's fine. I get that. Psych 101. It's—it's seeing myself see, seeing him see. It's seeing sight. It's thinking that my eye isn't me. That it has no personality. That it's anonymous. That my eye wonders who I am—." We walked past a row of figureheads leaning out from the wall: an Indian chief, a mermaid, a

Puritan woman holding a Bible to her chest, a griffin with glass eyes. "It's being incomplete, asking 'who?' when you think you're saying 'me.'"

"And?"

"And I could be anyone."

"But you're not anyone. You're *you*. Lydia, astronomer, teacher. Lydia with a freckle on her eyelid."

We'd walked up a set of stairs hardly noticing the steps and into the hall where the special collections hang.

"I've seen that look before, that look of looking, blank and not blank." Lydia paused, smiled at me—a strange, inexplicable smile, the smile someone gives you before telling you they're ill. "My first summer home from college I had taken to practicing the violin in the attic at night. My father thought I was doing it to be dramatic, to be an *artiste*. But I played in the attic to be in the only place in the house that felt unfinished, unformed. I went to play among all the things that through the years had been discarded. The violin, I knew, was something I was going to discard. I was going to get rid of the life I was supposed to live, stuff it in a trunk, let the moths live on it, not me. My father—he would sit on the top of the steps and listen. One night, practicing the same piece over and over again, Vinteuil's *Sonata,* the little theme, I kept missing a note—something I almost never did—missing a note in the simplest theme. The attic window was dark and the stars were coming out. I remember Venus so bright—that's

strange, isn't it? to remember Venus so bright? My father
came up. He looked at me like he was looking at his
looking at me. He looked at me this way, you know, this
certain way—and as he looked at me I told him I was
done, done with it, the violin. That violin, I remember
it. I remember the weight of it in my hand. It was an
heirloom. In it, my father would say, is the music my
ancestors played. My grandfather played it. My father
gave it to me on my thirteenth birthday. When I told
him—told him I was done, done with music—he
looked at me, looked at his looking at me, walked up to
me, took the violin in his hand, and smashed it against
the floor, once, twice, until it shattered, junk among the
junk, and he turned around, didn't say a word, walked
away and never mentioned music to me again. I looked
out the window. I could see my own face in it—that
same look. Looking at myself to see who I was. And
then I looked through me, and there was Venus, cloudy
Venus, and I heard the sound of the broken strings still
humming in the air, against the rafters, slowly dying but
singing still."

"How did you feel?" I asked.

"I felt proud."

I didn't know what to say. I just took her hand and
walked through the large doorway—so large it was as if
a wall had been removed to form it—around the parti-
tion with the artist's name reproduced in large vinyl letters, replicating his own handwriting, G. Moreau, to find
before us two paintings. One painting showed a man,

quite feminine in appearance, lower body wrapped in blue cloth, head bent in mourning, left hand raised over and behind him, holding on to the broken dead limb of a broken dead tree, and a cloth or veil numinous and ghostly behind his hand, hanging from the tree or from his fingers, a veil that in its semitranslucence also took shape, an owl or the spirit of an owl. The full moon—or is it the sun?—impossibly in front of the dark red trees. A mausoleum behind him. The man looked almost serpentine, holding in his other hand a flower he bent his head toward, not to smell it, but as if to press it against his forehead, to press it against the place of memory. Below him a dark patch—water, or hole, shadow from some unseen immensity, passage to the underworld.

In the other painting a woman with ivy twined in her hair, dressed in luxuriant prints, arabesque and oriental, looking down at the shield she cradled in her arms on which—eyes closed, mouth slightly open, head garlanded in laurel—a man's severed head rests. It was the head of the man from the other canvas.

"They are both paintings of Orpheus," Lydia said. "*Orpheus at the Tomb of Eurydice* and *Young Thracian Woman Carrying the Head of Orpheus.*"

"I know. I mean, I know the story. My father—for a long time—was concerned with Orpheus, his myth. 'Concerned' might be too light a word to describe it. He often told me about Orpheus at night before bed; he wrote me letters about Orpheus."

"Why?"

"That's a long story. I'm not sure I really understand *why* myself. Orpheus, he was a singer, a singer whose song was so beautiful not only people would be helpless to listen, but stones, trees, flowers. This meant something to my dad. Eurydice was the woman he loved and she died, bit by a snake on their wedding day, and Orpheus sang his way into the underworld to rescue her from death. And this meant something to him, too. It meant everything to him. Eurydice would follow him as long as he didn't look back—his song had to do his looking for him. But he did look back, and she fell back into the shadows, back into death." Then, looking at the second painting, "And the god-crazed women, years later, the maenads, they struck off his head, which sang as it fell through the air. Like your violin. Singing as it died."

I felt, I should say, very sad. I thought about my father; I imagined him in my head, but where his face should be I saw a mirror; I saw myself looking at him, my face on his body looking back at me, my eye etching an eye on the glass.

"Let's go, Lydia. I've had enough art for the day. And there's something I'd like to show you, something at the house, an old book that meant much to me."

"What's the book?"

"A book of wonders."

We retraced our steps through the museum. We walked by a gallery full of commotion. An elderly man had fallen down; his glass-topped cane lay in the middle of the room. A group of people gathered behind him, a sort of semicircle, almost as if he were a docent pointing out the details of a masterpiece; one woman let him rest back against her. He was pointing up at a painting, a view of a city by a river or lake—I could only see it for a moment, just out the corner of my eye—and saying in a feeble voice, nonetheless quite loud, "little patch of yellow wall, little patch of yellow wall." And then the man was gone, the scene erased, and we stepped out into the late summer's yellow light. How is it that dusk begins gathering in the trees before the sky? But so it is. Lydia walked down the steps and didn't look back; I kept turning around to see who might be following.

CHAPTER 4

"Your mother was so pretty. it's a shame she's not looking up at the camera," Lydia said, looking at the photo in the hall.

"I spent a lot of time as a boy looking at that picture, trying to remember her face. Sometimes I still try, but her face seems to be behind a veil, a veil the wind sometimes pushes against her face's shape. A cloth floating in the air, the shape always changing. I think as a boy I could remember it better, that she was more present to me. Still almost alive. My father took the photo down one day. I suppose it was painful for him to see it. The wall had a whiter square where the frame had been. I stared at it and cried, as if her face were still there, until he put it back."

"It sounds like such a lonely childhood."

"Maybe. I don't know. Maybe it was. I read a lot. My father encouraged me to do so, of course. It gave him time to work. I would sit under his desk, leaning back against his legs, reading." We walked down the hall to the study. "And when he wasn't working on the scroll, when he was out in the yard, or teaching, or cooking dinner, I'd sneak into the study and read a book on the shelf I was not allowed to read, a book of old fairy tales, dark tales and strange wonders. It would give me nightmares.

It frightened me. But I loved it. It made me feel closer to something I felt *in* me but could find no words for—it explained something about the world no one would talk about to me—"

"Your mother's dying?"

"Probably, yes." Lydia's saying that phrase, saying it so simply, so directly, affected me. My mother had not ceased to die. I felt like the little boy I had not ceased to be—that continuous child inside the adult who wanders through the labyrinth of his grown-up self, lost, afraid of monsters, afraid to speak too loudly lest his own words reveal him, and put him in greater danger, put him in the hands of the monster he asks for help to avoid.

"And the book? How did you find it?"

"Once upon a time," I thought a joke would change my mood, "I walked into the study and found my father leaning against the wall by the window reading a book with a green cover. When I came in he quickly closed it; I remember still the sound of his clapping it shut. He put the book in an open space on the lowest shelf and told me that it was a book I wasn't allowed to read. It was the only green book on the shelf, surrounded by drab black and brown leather spines of uninteresting others. It looked like a fresh sprig in blasted ground. I couldn't stop staring at it, noticing it every time I walked into his office. It had a sort of gravitational pull on me."

"It sounds like he wanted you to read it."

"What do you mean?"

"That he made such a show of it so that you'd feel tempted to read it, put it on the lowest shelf so you could reach it; he made it obvious which book you were forbidden to open."

We walked into the study. There on the desk the novel thickly sat—thought it was not so thick, then. One hundred pages, maybe less. There on the desk sat the novel's thick promise. I opened a drawer and pulled from it the sheaf of letters my father wrote me from his trip. I put them on the desk and pulled out the chair for Lydia to sit down.

"I thought you might want to read these. You don't have to—"

"What are they?"

"These are the letters my father wrote me from a long trip he took."

Lydia untied the ribbon holding them together and opened the first envelope.

I left her alone to read them. I didn't want to see her face as she read the letters; I didn't want to hover ghost-like over the ghosts those letters were to me. I walked to the kitchen to open a bottle of wine, poured myself a glass, the bouquet sudden and diffuse in the room when I took my first sip, sat in a chair, and stared at the wall while I waited. A blank wall gives the mind more fully over to its distraction, a movie with no plot cast through the eyes onto the screen, edited by images that repeat, as the glass of wine in my hand became another evening, a moment forgotten from last spring, when at Olin's house, slightly drunk, I knocked an empty wineglass off the table and it shattered against the floor and Lydia, looking down at the shards of glass on the wood, tipsily said, "That's how it begins."

When the glass was empty, I filled it again. I filled one for Lydia, and took it to her. She put down the last letter, placed it neatly on top of the others, and left them face down on the desk. "Your father thought he was Orpheus."

"I think he thought everyone was Orpheus. Or that Orpheus was some unrealized potential in us all. To be a singer. To sing a song that opened a door into another world. He thought of words as passages, not meanings; doorways, not definitions. He thought words kept open the wall between the living and the dead. I think he thought one could escape through a word. And enter. If he could sing the right words in the right order, sing them in the right way, some kind of multiplying melody, then he could sing his way into death and bring home my mother and sister. He was convinced, you know. He was absolutely convinced. He thought Orpheus wasn't a man but a symbol, a type of us all. Orpheus was who one could be—" I stopped, aghast to sound so much like him.

"It's hard to believe *he* could believe such a thing. A professor, a rational man. Your mother's death must have broken something in him."

"Reason's plank."

Lydia looked at me. "You had a hard childhood, not just a lonely one."

"A child doesn't know it's hard; I didn't. It was dark, that's all. Filled with shadows, mysteries. I loved my father very much. I loved him more the crazier he became. I thought he was magical. And wise. I'd listen to him practice the myth, practice his singing, his chanting, an awful music that hardly sounded like music, dark and rhythmic, guttural, almost violent—but it didn't scare me, or it scared me in a way that made sense, and so it didn't scare me. I didn't know to be afraid of the way he was crazy."

"And then he left?"

"And then one day he was gone."

"Weren't you angry?"

"I knew it would happen. He never told me he would leave, but I knew it. I knew he was practicing, preparing for a journey. The words he studied, I knew they meant he'd leave. I wasn't angry, I wasn't even surprised. Sad, I guess—I was already sad."

Something quiet in Lydia's face grew quieter; her whole face silence. "Fathers are an awful fate." Her face looked ashen.

"Fathers are just an introduction to fate; it becomes awful afterward, when fate is what you try to escape."

"What is your fate?"

I ignored the question. "My father came home a different man. He never spoke of what happened on that island. He would look at me in a way that I felt I could not ask him. It was secret." I thought about fate, how one doesn't know what it is, but only that it must be run away from, fled, and that fleeing it is always running directly toward it. "Father came home with a limp. His skin seemed more taut against him, as if he had been partially embalmed. He had a slightly jaundiced look. He kept teaching, but it didn't go well. He seemed as feeble as he actually was. He . . . dwindled. And then he died."

"I'm sorry."

Those three syllables rebounded through my head, a drumbeat repeating itself, growing louder as the words disappeared. The white poplar scratched against the window, pen on glass. I wanted to be able to say *don't be sorry* but I couldn't. I couldn't lie to her. "What I wanted to show you," trying to gather myself, trying to still the quaver in my words, "was the book, the green book, filled with tales. My childhood friend." I went over to the bookshelf. My hand by old habit reached to the middle of the lowest shelf, but the book was missing. It was gone. "It's vanished," I said, a desperate helplessness uncontrollable in my voice. *Vanished* is how the moment felt to me—not that I had lost the book, not that I had been reading it in the armchair and left it on a table in the living room, not that I had lent it to a friend or student and simply forgotten the fact. Orpheus had peeled himself off the canvas and stolen the book to keep his lonely head company in the afterlife—he had carried it away in his mouth. No natural explanations came to me;

I felt riddled, not as by a child's riddle book, but riddled as in filled with holes. "It's vanished, it's vanished—" I kept saying it to myself over and over again, and the empty space on the shelf opened the empty space in me, that absent space, as shocking as reading a novel and finding, hundreds of pages deep, a signature of blank pages, a missing chapter, after which the novel continues, missing characters one had come to like, to rely on, even to love. My hand was shaking, still held out toward the shelf. Lydia came behind me. She put her hand on my shaking hand, but the tremor didn't stop, it just descended deeper in me—more pressure in the fault of my earthquake life. She leaned her forehead against the back of my neck and said, "I won't vanish." She said these words but I could not see her say them; I could not see her eyes; I could not see her lips form the words. She spoke them behind me, as if the words existed in the air by themselves, spoken by anyone, anonymous. I wanted to say it, but I could not say it. I could not say it, but I knew it was true. Everyone vanishes.

CHAPTER 5

WHEN THE TENSES SHIFT, WHEN THE TENSES BLEND, memory stitches into yesterday's stitch, and time cinches shut. Not only shut. It loosens, frays. The Fates clap their hands in glee. The mind's loose hem dragging behind it across the ground, catching the salvage in the selvage: leaf's underside, light on water, a single lost pearl. A day repeats its pattern unexpectedly: the bee climbs in the bluebell that vibrates with its tune, the train's horn enters the tunnel; the hail crushes the mint, the scent of her hair when she pulls out the pin; frost on the window, sun's chromatic circles through the camera's lens. Echo chamber filled with words fills with words again; Narcissus looking out his eyes to see in the pond his eyes. No words can keep him from drowning. We cannot speak to ourselves and wake ourselves up, these words we say to ourselves that are the same words everyone speaks to themselves, these words in us but not our own, words that can describe the butterfly's plashless flight between the rose blossoms, words that can describe the butterfly's tattered wing torn by the rosebush's thorns; we speak them, but they will not wake us up, they will not stop us from bending down our mouths to the water to kiss our own reflection. Who is this *I* who says *I*? Who saying *I* thinks *I*? Who is this poor mirror-self who walks down the department hall so eerily quiet in the summer months, no sound of the copier machine endlessly repeating pages, no partially open doors from which voices escape in protest or explanation, no proliferation of endless detail, a girl's voice saying "the worm rapes the rose," no weary voice in return saying, "no, no——." Only the sound of my keys knocking against each other as I take them from my pocket, only the countless repetition of putting the key in the lock, of turning the key, of the rusty mechanism working once again, of the door opening, of the stifling air rushing into the cooler hall, of the feeling in my eyes at seeing my desk in its perfect order, in seeing my window, the glance of green through the pane, of the bookshelf, only the same weight in my eyes of knowing it all in advance, of seeing again what has been seen before, fate revealing itself in repetition, the copier machine of fate.

My mind—it is an exuberance of distraction. I cannot help it, when I hear out on the green a dog barking as it anxiously waits for the young woman to throw the blue disc across the lawn's expanse, I see without seeing poor Bitsy collapsed on the floor and hear what in my chair's voice was no doubt the nervous seed of a tone whose tendrils latch on only to grief; then I hear again as I heard before the dogs on my block yelping, howling, a canine frenzy affecting each, and looking out the front window, seeing a fox trot—wary but somehow calm in its wariness—down the center of the street; and its orange tail that ends in a dark tip . . . a sunset, but when did it occur? What plot was it part of? What chapter in what book? A poem in which a dog lies down across the sky? The fox, I remember it; it ran down the middle of the street, leisurely, looking from side to side; and then I remember the sunset, that sunset, that summer; I remember that sunset pouring itself through the open window of the hotel room, Lydia standing up naked from the bed and running quickly but languidly in front of the window, one arm almost covering her breasts, looking outside as she went by, looking back over her shoulder as she fled, or seemed to flee, down the carpeted hall that made her escape silent.

I sat down at my desk to read over the last pages of *Moby-Dick* I soon had to teach but the pages were blank. My eye couldn't see the words. Lydia's naked body kept walking past the window; on one page I was in the room she was in, and on the next page I was watching her body move past the window as I stood outside.

It was her idea. To get away before the academic year began. "A long weekend on the coast," she said. "It will do us good." I didn't especially like to travel, finding it hard to sleep in rooms other than my own, the noises and scents, even the feeling of the air that makes the foreignness of sleep more foreign, more threatening, removing the comfort of waking up to a room one recognizes before one recalls that one is oneself, that this room is familiar because it is mine, and if it is mine, then I must be me. But I agreed; I was in love.

Lydia planned everything. She picked the town and the hotel, and we drove off in her old convertible through the countryside for hours and hours, listening to music that the air rushing by made almost indiscernible, not talking; no need to talk, until a new music interposed, and hearing it before we saw it, we drove over a rise, and the ocean stretched beyond us to the horizon line; a line the eye draws to convince the mind the world has an edge just as a page has an edge, the waves crashing against the pebbled beach sending out to us its predictable crescendo, its pulse that roars.

"The brine in the air . . . do you smell it? It reminds me of being a little girl." Nostalgia filled Lydia's voice. She turned the music down but still spoke loudly.

"But you didn't grow up by the sea."

"I know. But it reminds me of being a little girl anyway. That air," she breathed deeply, "that makes possibility into a scent. What can't happen?" and she laughed, and taking one hand off the wheel, let the air sift through her fingers as she raised her arm above her.

The seaside town took a picture of itself printed on postcards in the spinning displays on the sidewalks outside the "General Store" and again outside the "Olde Tyme Shoppe," where one could buy polished stones, three dollars a bag. In the window of the taffy store the taffy machine churned away, two arms rotating around each other, the candy a milky white band in an oblong circle always threatening to break and fall on the ground or fling itself against a wall, but miraculously never breaking, the thinnest strands swept back into the machine's motion, so that children outside the window stood with their mouths agog while their soft-serve melted, dripping down their filthy fingers onto their toes. T-shirt shops: 1 for $12, 2 for $20, 3 for $25. We strolled through the town hand in hand. Lydia seemed transported by the very things that struck me as tawdry, dazzled by the glitter on the faces of children walking through the streets with butterflies painted on their cheeks; she saw beauty where I saw none, had convinced myself none existed—the trinkets in the trinket shop: toy slot machines, UFO tops with lights that flashed as they spun, candy rings with cherry-ruby gems . . . She'd wander into stores and browse, not to buy, but to wonder, or feel wonder, a childlike gaze that made the miniature replicas of the town's two-story church and the "rare" green stones found along the coast marvels of the lost world. She held my hand like I was one of the marvels, as if I were included; and so I began to see as she saw. We walked past a watch-repair store (the sign read PETER'S WATCH—& *Doll*—REPAIR) in whose front window dozens of pocket watches hung, no two telling the same time. One of the watches was turned around so that the face couldn't be seen, and etched into its brass back in an unsteady, amateur line, a fox asleep in the curve of its tail, the long grass of the field curling over it.

Lydia caught me gazing at it. "I'm going to buy it for you," she said.

A bell rang when she opened the door. The owner of the store looked up from behind the counter where he sat working, a small magnifying lens attached to his glasses, making his eye look as if it were detached from his head, floating in space.

"May I help you?" he asked in a tone surprisingly mechanical.

"I'd like to buy one of the watches in the window, the one with the fox engraved on the back." She turned around and pointed at the only watch whose face could be seen. A cacophony of ticking filled the store, each watch and clock marking the seconds for itself, each keeping time in its own world. I felt caught—not *in* time, but *in between* time. Each watch counted the hours off one by one, each case remembering the hand that had held it, the hand whose mortality the clock marked second by second until the hand existed no more, but the clock still did, adding up the math of nobody's demise. On a high shelf a row of dolls. One sitting stiffly in a crinoline pinafore stared down with only one blue eye open.

"I haven't repaired that one yet; it doesn't work."

Lydia smiled. "That's fine. It doesn't matter." And kissing me on the cheek, said, "He doesn't believe in time anyway."

A look of disgust passed over the man's face. Moving from behind the counter, he walked over to the window display, his legs so bowed that he teetered from side-to-side as he walked, the gait of a child's toy, an automaton. He took the watch down, held it in his palm, and with a look of disgust said, "Ten dollars."

"Is that all?"

"That's the worth of the metal. This watch can't be fixed. It was built by a hobbyist, just a kid fooling around. He thought he could devise a new mechanism that kept its motion perpetually. Foolish kid." He spat the words out in disgust. "It doesn't work."

Lydia handed him a ten-dollar bill and we left the store, the bell ringing at our departure.

"To the boardwalk," Lydia said, dragging me by the hand. The day was getting late and the sun was setting. Keeping time to my pace if to nothing else, the pocket watch struck my thigh with every step, a rhythm that made me more conscious of the moment, of holding Lydia's hand, of her hair swinging in front of her face and hiding it, of the neon lights' glow in the growing dark as we neared the boardwalk, where carnival rides and games grew illuminated in garish colors, sulfurous yellows within which barkers stood yelling out "three chances for three dollars, win your lady a prize!" in rapid-fire staccato, each more intent on marking his territory out from the men running other booths—throw a token onto a floating boat to win, shoot the water pistol into the clown's open mouth and win, arm wrestle the robot and win—than in having a customer actually stop and play. Pinball machines clanged and jingled, the spinning numbers clicked into high scores. A child walked by eating cotton candy, his mouth smeared with globs of pink that made his lips look almost blood smeared in the nauseous yellow light.

"Win me something." Lydia looked at me with eyes exaggeratedly imploring.

I walked over to the ticket booth. The man selling the tickets wore a banker's visor whose transparent green plastic cast a green shadow across his face. He was very tall, and leaned out his window toward me, and in a loud, slow voice, asked, "May I help you?"

"Five tickets, please." I gave him five dollars.

He took the money and put it in the cashbox, then counted off five tickets from a huge roll, "one, two, three, four," crimping each along its perforated line so that he was sure not to make a mistake, and reaching "five," tore them off. His hand shook slightly as he handed them to me. He had a tattoo on his arm whose faded ink made me realize that he was much older than I'd thought—a heart on fire and written in the flames the name Hazel. "The things kids do," he said, seeing me eye the mark, and then, pulling his shirt away from his neck, showed me a series of stars within whose constellation floated the name Beatrice. "You want to win your lady something? You do, don't ya?" I nodded. "Well, let me help you, Chief. Look here, Chief. Most these games you can't win, you just can't win 'em." He coughed into his hand. "You gotta pick right to impress the ladies. Go over there," pointing with a shaking arm to a booth from which red light poured glaringly out, "and give him three tickets," he held up three shaking fingers, "which gives you three balls. You gotta break two plates." He laughed to himself a sickly laugh, as if he were betraying a sacred code. "Oh, they play tricks, they do! They paint cracks on plates made of lead, they put chips in metal plates, make it look like they're gonna fall apart of themselves. Don't throw at those, no, don't throw at them." Lydia stood behind me, listening. "Look for the blue ones, and aim for those. They'll be furthest back, looks like they're the hardest to hit, like you shouldn't even try. But I tell you, Chief. If the ball even goes close to it the breeze will crack it in half." He winked at me, leaned closer, and said, "She's a looker. Win her a prize and if you're lucky you'll get lucky. It's a lucky night." His laugh turned into a cough almost indistinguishable from the laugh as we walked away.

"Virgil points me this way," I said, as we made our way through the crowd. A little girl with glasses stood still and cried, her lenses lit blue by the neon lights above her so her eyes couldn't be seen, just the blue trails of her tears streaking down her face. A woman ran to her, bent down, hugged her, and then smacked her behind. "Don't wander off like that! It's dangerous here! There are strange people!" and as she said this she glanced my way, as if I were the threat.

When we reached the booth I handed the man the tickets. He was wearing a flannel shirt with the sleeves torn off, a large gold necklace with a cross, and the long strands of his mullet kept getting caught in the whiskers of his unshaven face; with a surprisingly feminine motion, he kept pushing the hair back. "You sure don' look like you can win this lady a prize. Let me give you some advice, Boss, jus' a little advice. Look close and you'll see some of these plates ain't made so well. Jus' aim for 'em."

I took the first hard rubber ball, spotted a light blue plate in the back corner, wound up, and threw the ball hard, smacking it in the middle, and feeling an absurd pride as it smashed into hundreds of smithereens. Lydia squealed in joy. She jumped up and down clapping her hands.

"You might be impressin' your lady there, but you ain't impressin' me, Boss." He brushed some hair back off his face, an amused glint in his eye. "You gotta hit two out of three. Now looky there, that plate has a crack in it, that one right over there." But I'd spotted another blue plate in the opposite corner of the booth, drew my arm back, and threw it as hard as I could. But my aim was off, and the ball smacked into a large pink teddy bear with a heart emblazoned on its stomach, knocking it off the wall, a little puff of dust in the air after it fell. "Whoa, Boss! Whoa! Rein it in, Boss!" He squinted at me. "You sure don't take any advice, do you? You gotta do it your own way, don't you? You're strongheaded," and leaning out to see Lydia, "You got yourself a stubborn one here. You best watch out for this one. He's gonna hurt you. He's made of metal, this one is. He's made of stone."

Lydia put her hand on my shoulder, stood up on her toes, and whispered in my ear, "Let's go."

The carnival man heard her say it. "Boss, I hate to say it. I hate to tell this to you. But she don't think you can do it. She lost her confidence in you. She likes you and all. That's plain to see. But she thinks you're kind of— well, kind of weak. Can't follow through. She likes you and all. But, you know—she's got her doubts, she does. I see it in her eyes."

"Let's go, Daniel."

I threw the last ball up in the air and caught it as it fell back down, and in one fluid motion, drew my arm back, and sped the ball to the plate I'd just missed. The ball struck the plate's edge. It didn't break, didn't shatter. It spun on its stand like a flicked coin, wobbled as it lost its speed, and fell off the platform, shattering against the ground.

"I think, Boss," I said, looking at the man running the booth, "that this weak-armed man has won the lady a prize."

As we walked back through the crowd on the boardwalk Lydia examined her prize. She had picked a commemorative plate on which the town's portrait had been printed. It was dusk. The lights were coming on in the buildings. The Ferris wheel's lights were lit up in yellows and oranges and reds. The stars were coming out. Lydia kept gazing down at it. "It's not real," she said. "They aren't real." Her voice was sad.

"What's not real?"

"The stars. They're not real. They don't correspond. Someone just added in some dots."

There was a note of devastation in her voice. I didn't know what to do, what to say.

"It's only a plate." I knew it was the wrong thing to say even as I said it. But before Lydia could react, a siren broke the crowd apart. An ambulance drove down the middle of the boardwalk, a fish swimming upstream. It stopped by the ticket booth, and then we saw him, the man who had sold us the tickets, face down on the ground. A pudgy boy was crying. "He just fell over! He just fell over!" he kept saying to the paramedic. "He just fell over! It's not my fault!" An accordion roll of tickets dangled from his hand. "I didn't do anything! He just fell over!"

"He was just alive," Lydia said.

And before I could respond, she clutched her stomach, ran over to the side of the walk, bent over, and threw up.

"Lydia—" I helped her stand up. I put my arm around her, and walked her back to the hotel—the plate on which the stars were not stars held loosely in both her hands.

The minute hand clicked into place; I could hear it. I looked up from the page on which memory had printed itself in images over the words beneath it. 2:00. Class had already started. I grabbed my book and set off down the hall. *Minute hands, hour hands, the hands of the clock,* I thought as I walked quickly down the hall to the stairs. *Minute hands, hour hands, the hands of the clock.* We give time human hands. We give time open hands into which we fall. Comfortless comfort. I walked down the stairs deeper into memory.

The fluorescent bulb's medicinal light cut an angle across the carpet. Lydia left the bathroom door open, splashing cold water on her face, leaning down and drinking water straight from the faucet, and after rinsing her mouth spitting it out again. When she stepped out into the room dark circles under her eyes made her look more tired than I had ever seen her. She reached behind her and flicked the light off. Then the room was dark save for the light coming through the window, a pale light, the full moon's light, toward which Lydia walked, resting her forehead against the cool pane.

"Are you feeling better?" I asked, standing next to her, putting my arm on her shoulder.

"Look at that," she said, staring out the window, looking down the cliffside on which the hotel was perched, down to the ocean. "Look at the moonlight on the kelp bed." The moon's light, paler than pale, whiter than white, reflected on the water, whose surface rolled as matter rolls, thickened by the bed of kelp, a sodden blanket disintegrating in the ocean in which it had been abandoned, a body. The moonlight spread out on the surface, and as the kelp rolled with the ocean's rolling, would distend, would widen, would break into two bodies that merged in the next instant back into one. The moon looked like the ghost of the moon.

"You feeling better?"

"Yes . . . ," she kept her head against the glass, "no . . . ," watching the moon's reflected permutations endlessly undulate. "There's something I need to tell you, Daniel. I feel bad that I haven't told you."

I had this sudden fear that she was dying. I thought the moon was telling me that Lydia was dying and I couldn't look at it anymore. I went to the bed and sat down, but Lydia stayed at the window, as if watching the reflection of the moon's reflected light to find the words to say what she must say. "You're sick, aren't you? Don't tell me you're sick, please." I said these words to her as a child might say them.

"I'm not sick." A long time she looked down at the moon on the sea's imperfect mirror. In a strange voice, a voice distracted but enchanted, "I don't think I've ever seen the moon. But now I see it." Silence. "I'm not sick, Daniel. I'm pregnant." And at the last word she turned around to see me sitting on the bed looking at the floor.

"You are . . . are you sure?"

"I am."

Just those two words, those ancient words, sourceless or source of themselves, affirmative of everything, of person and place, of mind and matter, those most intimate words I have been at times in my life afraid to utter to myself lest they prove to be true or untrue, those words, two syllables, they broke open in me all that is their

opposite, all those who could say *I am* but now cannot;
those two syllables opened up in me that space in which
no syllables could be spoken, that airless world where the
moon is just another pearl lost in a box, the breathless
moon, the lightless moon, the moon that steals for itself
what looks like light, mirror made of stone that lights up
no face but its own; I stared at that moon in me, that
moon whose light lights nothing, that nothing in me
where my mother and my sister fell when I was but a
child, that dark nothing, darker than the night ocean's
depths, that other night the sun never brightens into
which my father ventured as if venturing into me and
returned from nothing with nothing as his reward. Lydia's
I am, those simple words expressing the impossible fact
not only of being alive but of carrying life within her—
they spoke to me only of life's opposite, as if the third syllable following the first two was a syllable in reverse, a *not*
so deeply not, so truly negative, its existence annulled its
own utterance.

"I am not a father. I can't be."

"You can, Daniel."

"I've told you. I can't bring someone into this world
only to leave it. Or be left."

"Daniel, life is—"

"Short, uncertain—and its opposite endless."

"Daniel—"

"No." I looked quickly up at her. She had a face that
was hers. Lydia's. The moon had no face behind her,
lower on the horizon. "No. No."

Lydia looked at me. I stared into the dark circles in the center of her eyes, those holes into which light pours. Mind and malady. She looked at me. And wordlessly, she took her bag from off the floor, took her keys from the wardrobe's top, and left.

I sat there in the silence she left behind. I'm still sitting there—where I let the woman I love disappear. I stood up. I pulled from my pocket the two tickets never spent and put them on the bedside table; I took the watch from my pocket. The fox upside down—falling through the grass in which it slept—unaware that it was falling.

CHAPTER 6

THE AWFUL INTIMACY OF THE CLASSROOM WEIGHED DOWN
on me and I felt myself blushing too—all the needless
exposure, speaking about what I think to people I don't
know. I stammered out, "I'm not your professor," which
brought uncomfortable laughter from most of the class, "but
for today I'll have to do." I looked down at my hand somehow surprised to see a book in it, and, horrified that I could
not gather myself into my professorial façade, blushed all the
more deeply as I walked behind the desk, put the book on
it, turned it in a half circle so it wouldn't be upside down,
and sat in the chair. A screech rose above the murmuring
voices as I inched my chair closer to the desk.

"I'm sorry to be late." I surveyed the students, most of
whom were looking down at their desks or at their hands
as if scrutinizing the palimpsest graffiti or their palms'
lines for a prophecy that would see them through the
next hour of their lives. One young man looked directly
at me, though. He had gray eyes. He held his right hand
heavily on the cover of his copy of *Moby-Dick* as if pro-
tecting it from whatever I might say. He looked quite
pale. "Are you feeling all right?" I asked him.

"Just waiting to begin." He said this with an edge of
recrimination in his voice that made the girl sitting next
to him ruefully smile. "I feel fine."

"Yes, well—let's begin. Open your books." Hundreds of pages being thumbed through to find the final chapters sounded like so many sighs. "Obviously, I haven't been privy to your previous conversations, nor to what approach your professor has guided you through to this"—looking down at the novel still closed before me—"whale of a book, or book of a whale"—tugging on my collar and then opening the book to the last fifty pages—"but I think I have a great privilege today," I looked up, "to talk about the end of my favorite book ever written—this awful, full-of-awe, end."

"We've taken a historical approach," a girl offered.

"Historical?"

"Biography, cultural context, reviews—you know, *history*." She said the word with a slight revulsion directed either at my own possible stupidity or at the word itself.

"I understand the term. My approach," taking a deep breath before the confession began, "is different. I'd simply like to talk about the book."

Another voice, faceless, from the back of the room. "Are you going to take attendance? I need to be here today to get credit for this course. My name is—"

"Please, stop. Don't tell me your name. We're going to be anonymous today. You don't get to know my name—and if you know it, please erase it from your head—and I don't get to know your names. I've marked everyone present already. You get to be 'you' when I ask you a question; you get to be 'I' when you answer. The same goes for me. We don't have to spend time trying to impress each other, or trying to be smart. You don't need to like me; I don't need to be impressed by you. We're free to say what we think."

The uncomfortable silence broken: "I think this is the worst book I've ever read. It's so boring." The young man who spoke seemed plainly proud of his honesty. His eyes peered out from the shade beneath his white baseball cap's filthy rim.

The class seemed to hold its breath, as if their peer had decided to test my own invitation to speak freely one's mind. "That's meaningless," I said, "without knowing what books you do like." I paused. "Even then, and forgive me for being so frank, but to find a book *boring* speaks, perhaps, to a lack of inner resources. Even boring books aren't boring. The people who read them are." I couldn't believe I said the words even as I said them.

The boy scowled at me. "It's irresponsible. It's crazy. It lets its plot dwindle to nothing so it can talk about how to chop up whales." And then, pausing before pushing further, "And the people who like it—they're the same. Irresponsible and crazy."

"Actually, they unwind the whale—like a scroll—before they chop it up. To just chop it up would be irresponsible. So much of the whale would be lost in the process." The boy with the gray eyes continued. "And I—I love those chapters."

"Of course you do" the scowler scowled. "You're—" and searching some seconds for the right word, spat it out: "predisposed."

"You just want to read a book where you get to turn the pages as quickly as you can." The gray-eyed boy didn't seem flustered; he seemed happy to settle into a conflict long overdue. "You want to be entertained."

"Yeah. I'd like to enjoy the books I read. Call me crazy."

"If you were crazy, you wouldn't need to enjoy something to think it mattered. You should work on being crazy. Everything is interesting to the crazy."

"Like Ahab?" Venom-voiced. "He killed his whole crew to chase a whale. He wasn't *interested* in *everything*. He didn't care about anyone."

The gray-eyed boy had a curious look on his face. "Ahab doesn't read books."

"What kind of answer is that?" The boy was furious, and visibly attempted to calm himself down. "What kind of answer is that? *Ahab isn't real.* Just like this class. Just like you. Not real."

The gray-eyed boy turned around and looked to the front of the class. "That's why you're no good at this—reading. You think you're smart, maybe you are. Who cares, though? Being smart doesn't help. You don't think anything's real that isn't real to you. All those chapters you hate, all that information about killing whales and processing them, they're beautiful. They're more dramatic than Ahab's chase. They make everything real. They make us part of it. They make it real to us and they make us real to it. You know why you want to be entertained?"

Disgustedly, "Why?"

"Because you have no imagination."

"Fuck you." And the boy stood up from his desk, slung his backpack over one shoulder, grabbed his book, and said, "I'm done with this class and your pretentious . . . all your pretentious shit." He dumped his copy of *Moby-Dick* in the trash can beside the door—one loud metallic thud rang out in the shocked silent room—and left.

Everyone in the class stared at me, save for the gray-eyed boy. He gazed out the window, watching the angry student cross the lawn at a clip, kicking off the head of a dead dandelion. I saw him do it; I looked out the window, too—looking aside so as to think for a moment, not to dispel the palpable tension in the class, but to feel it longer, this sense of open and wild expectation unclouded by each student knowing what word must come next, what point must be established, reaching a conclusion, getting to say what it is something "means"; the only sense was that something must happen, would happen.

I stood up and walked to the window. I didn't turn around, but I could feel the eyes of the class follow me, so that to see me was also to look out the window. Their classmate small in the distance had almost disappeared from sight. "There he goes," I said, "another orphan." It could have been a joke, but I didn't mean it as a joke, nor did I say it as one. And without turning around,

"Since I'm anonymous, and you all are anonymous, I think I'll make a small confession. I hate to lecture, and I'm tired of teaching—and I think I'll give it up. I didn't even prepare to teach all of you today. I've read this book more times than I can count, and I thought 'why prepare?' So I didn't. It makes one weary, you know? Thinking about what you think. Whether each one of you, or even just one of you, leaves a class—even a class I'm teaching—feeling 'fortified by education'—well, it's shameful to say (but I don't feel ashamed), but I don't think I care." If I couldn't see the class in the window's reflection, I would have thought the room empty. "What's-his-name, the one present in the attendance checklist alone, he kicked a dandelion head as he stormed across the lawn. A funny thing to notice, isn't it? I saw the cloud-puff of seeds when he did it. He kicked it in anger, anger at one of us, maybe at many of us, maybe at me, yes, but also at the book we haven't even yet talked about. That's fine. I feel angry, too. I don't know why I'm angry. This book—it isn't rational, it isn't reasonable, it incites emotion. Maybe his anger is a legitimate interpretation. I don't know. I do know that he kicked the weed—I *witnessed* it—and now despite him and his fury the seeds will float delicately, even beautifully, through the air (it's happening right now, even as I speak) and will eventually settle, and some will die, and some will take root, and some will grow and flower and go to seed again, and one of these, maybe more, maybe none, a child will pluck off its stem, and before blowing all the seeds away, that child will make a wish. Isn't it good your fellow classmate got so angry? Now a wish will come true." I turned around, somewhat surprised at the childish angle of my thought. "So, I'll make a wish, too. I'll be the child who makes a wish, and you can be the angels or monsters or fates or gods who grant it. Like every real wish, mine is a question, not a demand. I wish to know what you think about Ahab, what you think about Ishmael, and what happens to these two men, very different men but also much the same, at novel's end—which, I hopefully assume, all of you have read for today."

"I don't know what to think about Ahab," a girl who came to class in her jogging outfit said. "Part of me hates him. When I put down the book I hate him. I hate what he did to all those men. He seems so selfish. But when I'm reading he intrigues me. He's—magnetic."

"He is magnetic. He describes himself or his soul as a 'Leyden Jar.' He's magnetic, he's electric, but is he selfish?" I asked.

"I think so."

The gray-eyed boy spoke up. "Selfish isn't the right word. His absorption in himself is deeper than that. We're all selfish. Ahab is something different."

"Ahab is Ahab," I offered, walking back to the desk. "Ahab is forever Ahab. He reads the coin he nailed to the mast and in every symbol stamped on it he sees Ahab. Everyone on the ship is to him another Ahab. Only the white whale isn't him—" I paused, thinking—

"But part of him is in the whale. His leg——" The gray-eyed boy said, looking through his book for a passage.

"Ahab is over-complete and incomplete. He's not simply 'mad.' As he says himself, he is 'madness maddened.' He is too much and not enough."

A young man growing a scraggly beard beneath which a palpable shyness leaked out said, "If Ahab thought everyone was Ahab, then he didn't really kill them. He just killed himself."

The girl in the jogging suit: "But that ignores the horror of what he did. Dozens of men lived on that ship. And it was Ahab who led them to their deaths. They had wives and children . . ." her voice trailed off, imagining it, "and now their bodies are gone, lost at sea. No grave for anyone to visit, no——" and abruptly, she stopped speaking.

"They become anonymous again, death being a return, perhaps, to anonymity," I said, mindlessly turning pages of the book, looking down at none of them. "A strange correlate of that thought is that our class today, each of us being for an hour nameless, is having a deathly, deathlike conversation. Maybe we need to think of ourselves as in the water with the drowning whalers, the white whale swimming between us with our captain lashed to its giant body, and our speaking of these men, of what happened to them, of what never ceases to continue happening to them, gives them the only air left they can breathe. Maybe their lives are in our hands, and class isn't about learning anything at all, it's not even about reading a book—it's about," I waited for the word to come into my mouth, "resuscitation." The class was quiet, not distracted. "And the book begins in anonymity. 'Call me Ishmael.' All we know from the first sentence is that whoever it is that says 'I' in this book isn't named what he asks us to call him. He's anonymous, a self without a name, without the fate of a name, as if he has lived through his own death and been born again, born blank, and having no parents, this orphan, he must name himself. Ishmael—"

"Yes?" The gray-eyed boy looked up, as if out of a reverie, and then coming back to the present moment, looked abashed, and turned his eyes back to the book in front of him.

"More and more, I think about Ishmael at novel's end. Floating there in the ocean." I felt a surge of emotion in me I thought I must control. "Ishmael—but let's remember this is *before* he is Ishmael—floats there in the ocean, the infinite ocean, just as Pip had done before him, below the singular god above him in the sky, above the multitudinous god below him in the water, a single man, a mote, merely a mote, but not nothing. Is it hopeless or hopeful? I can't tell. He calls himself an orphan, but it's not only his family that's missing. It's everyone. It's everything. His name. The world. Here is the nameless, worldless man (think for a second how these two conditions always go together) with his arms around his friend's coffin. The coffin is all that keeps him alive. To stay alive, he puts his arms around death; this coffin that rose to the surface, buoyant because there is no body in it, only breath is in it, only air. That coffin—you'll all remember—is carved with the mystic markings tattooed on Queequeg's body, inked by the prophet on his skin, symbols Queequeg himself couldn't read—the secrets to the universe, the meaning of life. This coffin is a library," I felt a giddy exhaustion, "that cannot be read, self-enclosed. You cannot read what is in it, and yet it exists, and yet it is real. So many years I've taught students," looking up, "just like all of you. So many of you think you come here to learn something, that in these books, this book," holding it up in my hand, "there is some meaning you can read that will help you, that will be of use to you . . . but here is a book on your class's last day that denies any of that is true. You don't read a book. You don't learn something from it that will help you. You don't get smarter." A wellspring of feeling flooded up in me, a feeling that I could not help but say what I had to say—the very feeling I had spent years training myself to ignore, to tamp down, to refuse. "You don't read a book. You put your arms around it; and it saves you." I looked up at the class again. "Or it doesn't." Most of the students were looking down at their desks, looking at their hands. The gray-eyed boy stared at me, scrutinizing me. I felt in an uncanny way that I'd met him before, that we knew each other, but hadn't seen each other for years. The feeling didn't ease my mind, the tension of my mind—it did the opposite. The sense of familiarity, of not being wholly alone in my thinking, gave me more fully over to my abandon. "Ishmael. He ties the book's end into its beginning, a snake with its tail in its mouth. It is only his being so deeply orphan, no name, no world, no ability even to say 'I' as he floats on the ocean, lost to everything but the infinite fact of the world extending limitless past his poor self-shard that, years later (we don't know how many years intervene between the last page and the first, we only know the last page impossibly comes before the first page, and that time in the novel is backwards and because backwards is a version of fate—we read toward what has already occurred) he can say, or he *must* say, 'Call me Ishmael.'" I took a breath; I looked at the window as I walked over to it. "A book begins by defining 'Who I am'; it ends by asking 'Who am I?' We are allergic to the world; consciousness is an allergic reaction to the fact of the world; it is our understanding that is a form of irritation, a rewarding irritation, and we think, because we think, we have accomplished something noble, something valorous, that we can say what it is something means; but it is just a symptom of the allergy, the mind trying to rid itself of itself, of what enters it by casting it back out, words for world." The grass outside the window waved in the wind. "But this book, our book, it ends before the book it is has been written. We end at the wordless beginning, when the whole world is unspeakable, unknown, and all capacity to make use of it, to turn it into something that feels like it means something, is gone. We ourselves are survivors. Everyone we know is drowning below us, is already dead. The world is an awful, undeniable fact. But we survive—lucky us—we survive. We are the ones who remember. We must relearn our names or give ourselves new ones. We must keep our arms around the book to survive." I leaned my forehead against the cool glass. I breathed deeply, slowly, deliberately. My heart raced. "Ahab—I think he knew this. And the young gentleman in class is right. Ahab doesn't read books. He doesn't want to read books because he doesn't want to survive. Ahab wants the opposite, our awful hero. Ahab—he had a question about death that he could only ask to death itself, and if that required dying, well, then he'd die. Isn't Ahab also Ahab in death? Isn't that his terrible question? And if he is Ahab isn't he captain still to all his crew? All his dead crew? Can't he, even in death, gather them again, and put them within the mystery of his command? Ahab knew another world hid darkly behind this bright one, and in that ancient quest, as every hero must, he found a way to thrust himself into the dark world where living and dying aren't opposites." I closed my eyes. "A book and a whale—both of them, it seems, are more than themselves. They resemble each other, not perfectly. A white page and a white whale. Both are passageways into the wider world, where death is an end that does not end, is different than we expect, where death may be deathlike, or not death at all. The book and the whale—they are the death that is an event of life, they are the death one lives through."

I stood with my head against the windowpane, eyes closed, and stayed silent. After a few minutes I heard the students leaving, one by one. And when I thought the room was empty, I opened my eyes, looked briefly outside at the green, green grass, and turned around. I thought I would be alone, but I wasn't. The gray-eyed boy still sat in his desk, looking at me.

"Thank you for this class," he said.

"I don't know if I'd thank me for it," I said.

He looked directly at me, not affected by my own exhausted awkwardness. "No," he said. "Thank you." He didn't speak for a while, only looked at me in a way few people ever looked at me. He looked at me—the thought suddenly occurred to me, the concise nature of all the acute strangeness gathering around this boy all afternoon—as I looked at myself. He had—I thought with confusion bordering on horror—my own eyes. "What are you teaching in the fall?" he asked.

"A new class. It's called Wonderful Investigations."

"Good. I'll sign up."

Gathering myself, I said, "Then tell me your name. I'll keep lookout."

"Call me Ishmael," he said.

I laughed.

"No, really," he said. "My name is Ishmael."

CHAPTER 7

I WALKED HOME PAST THE APPLE TREES' ABSENCE, PAST
the flowers missing yearly, past the vanished scent
that would step bodily out the leaves when the wind
blew; I walked past the branchless, fruitless, branches and
fruit. I walked past everything that was missing, thinking
about the angry student stomping off through the grass,
watching him disappear through the classroom window.
I could still hear the sound of the novel hitting the trash
can's metal bottom, like a dull hammer's thud when the
nail is already deep in the wood; that book now sat next
to mine in my bag. I had pulled it out, leafed through it.
The student said he hated the book, but almost every
page contained an underlined sentence, often more than
one, and in a restrained and neat hand, questions filled
the margins. A blue line so straight it must have been
made with a ruler underscored *That same infinitely thin,
isinglass substance, which, I admit, invests the entire body of the
whale, is not so much to be regarded as the skin of the creature,
as the skin of the skin, so to speak; for it were simply ridicu-
lous to say, that the proper skin of the tremendous whale is
thinner and more tender than the skin of a new-born child,*
after which an arrow cut from sentence's end back
through the underlined words, to a passage above, *and
being laid upon the printed page, I have sometimes pleased*

myself with fancying it exerted a magnifying influence. In the margin he precisely wrote *the monster's skin; or the impossible magnifying glass.* The page dissects the monster, and the monster magnifies the page; the monster forces us not to flee but to pay attention. I thought about the pages of my own novel, splayed around the circle of the trash can's edge, looking as if they were forever being sucked down into a whirlpool; but the whirlpool didn't whirl, it just collected dust; at the center of it, I thought, the monster lives. Every father is a monster.

One cannot run away from what one thinks. It follows. From it there is no escape. The minotaur in the labyrinth lives in the center whorl of the thumb's print, of every finger's print that leaves its guilty stain on everything touched, its inky stain on the page; it lives in the center of guilt but is not guilty itself, the monster; no, I am always the guilty one; haunted by ghosts I ask to haunt me, hearing laughter in the wind, laughter in the wind in the trees, eating toast in the kitchen in the dark, dry burnt toast, and finding the crumbs in the morning tracing my path across the floor. My father left me. I wrote him into pages and threw the pages away so I could leave him. Pathetic. The monster says one word in a thousand voices: source. At the beginning, there is a monster. He cannot be killed by killing him, cannot die by being dead. To invoke him, say "I." Look in the mirror and say "I" over and over again until your own face goes blurry, say "I" until your eyes fail, and say it still until "I" fails, until it means nothing, until it is a syllable as meaningless as the waterdrop dripping from the faucet. Then you'll see him. Then the fingerprint's whorl becomes a noose around the monster's neck; but the same noose is around my neck. I am the other. Poets sing it, but it isn't a song. There is no *Song of Myself*. There is only a hiss, I can hear it now hissing in me, as of lips straining not to let go the last taken breath. Lydia said she'd heard it, the hissing edge of the world, the hissing static of the edge. It's every lost voice speaking at once.

Though I never lock it, I put the key into the front door's knob and turned it. All this useless chatter with myself, I thought, sick of myself talking to myself, of the endless repetition of the same thoughts accusing each other of impotence. I pushed hard on the door, but it didn't budge; I pushed harder and harder, shaking the door by the knob until the glass rattled, pounding the door with my fist, knocking my knuckles against it again and again until the skin felt raw and bleeding over the bone; knocking as if inside the house there might be someone living in it to let me in, someone deeply, irretrievably asleep. I'd locked myself out. I sat down on my knees on the stoop, looking at the door all the people I'd ever loved had walked through countless times, looking at the knob their hands had clasped; I leaned my head against the wood and cried. I couldn't help it. I'd locked myself out; and I'd locked myself in. I was a book on a shelf locked behind the glass watching people pass, watching Lydia pass, and stop, and peer in to read the titles, Lydia pregnant with my child—. I leaned my head against the door and cried, the house rising out from my forehead like some projection of my innermost thoughts, my intimate thoughts, my home thoughts in which I could live with those I love—the more-than-real house that confuses the head and heart into one pulsing room, that nervous house where the mother and sister I lost to death still live, still go about their lives, missing me without knowing what me they're missing. That was the house whose door I locked against myself; that was the door against which I leaned my head and cried.

I sat back and looked at the knob, the key like a knife stuck in a stone. I reached up and turned it. I stood up. I took out the key and put it in my pocket. I grasped the knob and opened the door, which swung smooth on its hinges. I walked into the cooler air. My mother's picture hung on the wall. I put my finger to her face and touched her, and a moist fingerprint remained when I took my hand away, slowly evaporating as I watched. My mother sat in the middle of my own face—my face reflected in the picture's glass. I couldn't have guessed it—that I must choose, must daily make a choice. That I must pull myself off the shelf and open myself up to be read. That I was the green book filled with wonders, the forbidden book not truly forbidden, the vanished green book—that was me, and I was missing, had been missing, from my own life, for years. The thought struck me as absurdly dramatic, the sort of epiphanic moment I might come across in a novel and put the book down in jaded dismay.

I called Olin.

"Hello?" He answered on the fourth ring. I could hear a scraping sound in the background. "Hello?," he added a second time, hastily.

"It's Daniel." My voice sounded to my own ears strained by the emotion I had tried to calm down before calling. "I haven't called at a bad time?"

"Oh, Daniel, hello. I thought you were calling to offer me a deal on having my air ducts cleaned or extending my car warranty. They always call when I'm in the kitchen."

"Are you cooking?"

"I'm right now stirring the chocolate as it melts. Trying to keep it from burning. A hero's labor."

"Well, it's good you're a hero, then." It felt hard to joke, releasing a pressure in me I did not want to ease.

"Yes. I'm a cake hero. I'm making a mythic choco-late cake to fortify me as I journey to the world of the shades to seek advice from—"

"Olin," I cut him off midsentence, "I have a favor to ask—a somewhat strange one."

"Those are my favorites. The stranger, the better."

"Could you meet at the Old Library at sunset?"

"It sounds like a Western. Is there a showdown? Student disagree with his grade? Department not big enough for the two of you? Or is it a Romance? You're not—are you, Daniel?—trying to seduce me? Not again. I've told you, I'm devoted to my abstemious life, a life of ascetic restraint and monk-like contemplation. Well, what genre is it? Tell me, so I know how to dress."

"The genre is Crime."

"Wonderful!" I heard the ice clink in the glass as he took a sip. "I am dashing in black. Black flatters me."

Olin was waiting for me on the steps when I arrived. The setting sun lit up a cloud that leaned over the whole sky like a pink sail pulling the earth into the harborless night. He was dressed all in black: black jeans and long-sleeved black T-shirt. He smiled as I walked up the steps; he put his hand on my shoulder and looked me keenly in the eye and smiled. I thought he'd make a joke, dispel the oddity of meeting like this with his wit that made light of anything burdened by mystery. But he didn't. He only squeezed my shoulder twice, and arched his eyebrows over his eyes, which opened wide, a look of almost child-ish anticipation; but a look, too, of childish wisdom, as of seeing something for the first time, a spider gently tap-ping the back of the wasp entangled in its net.

We went inside. The heat of the dying day hung in the air, a stifling dry heat that lent an otherworldly quality to the moment, as if we had stepped into a new atmosphere of a ruined world whose sun had ravaged the planet. The bottom floor of the Old Library was used for storage now that the college had built the multiangled, titanium-sheathed monstrosity that is the new library. The dust was lit by the pink light leaking through the windows. Empty shelves leaned against each other, invalids in the sanato-rium. White sheets covered large tables. A broken lamp splayed across the floor, its green glass shade in shards around it. We walked up the stairs to the room where rare books were still kept, the room in which the chair throws his yearly parties, a room still infused with that fading grandeur of the century past, a room still dressed in time. Pan leered down from the ceiling, the old god cast in plaster. Venus bright in the purpling dusk, the moon a rubble cup above it. The sky floated in front of the books behind the glass. I walked up to it and saw myself grow larger as I neared, the light in the room too dim to reflect anything more than a featureless shadow. Olin's shadow followed behind mine. The green book sat on the shelf, absorbing what light remained into itself so that in the darkening room it seemed to dully glow. I put my hand against the glass, so strangely cool to the touch. I pulled on the small brass handle but the case was locked. Olin braced the shelf against the wall, putting his weight against the wooden frame. And when he had steadied himself, a human buttress aslant, I yanked the handle with all the strength I could muster; it felt at first as if nothing had happened, as if the lock had withstood the force exerted against it, as if my muscle and my will had no power over it, as if it were a substance other than metal and glass and wood, subject to other laws than my meager force; and then, the small lock burst apart, the inner mechanism springing open and scattering across the floor, the brass pins and springs caught in the fringe of the thick rug in the center of the dark floor.

I took the book off the shelf. The day's heat had

warmed the green leather; it was as hot as another hand in my hand, but denser. Perhaps it was because what I had just done was illicit, even wrong, that I felt as I did; but holding the dense, warm book in my hand I felt my senses not swoon but heighten, each gaining a specificity my mind could not decipher—I heard the crickets begin their song, and hearing it I heard the violins play that in this room had played so many months ago, in my mouth the taste of wine long ago swallowed, and in my hand Lydia's hand, Lydia's hair, the scent of her hair, the hail-crushed mangle of battered mint, her hair. I bit my lip. I heard my father's footsteps in Olin's footsteps as he walked across the floor, gathered the pieces from the broken lock, and carrying them back to the open shelf, put them in a neat pile in the gap left by the missing book. I walked to the doorway and looked back to see Olin wiping with a brilliant white cloth our fingerprints from the glass.

He looked over at me and waved. I thought I could see a sorrowful look on his face, but his face was hard to see in the night, now that night had filled the room.

I walked down the stairs and out into the night, clutching the book against my chest. I could feel my heart beat against it. I held it to me as a mother might hold a child to her breast as she fled a danger. But I was the danger I was fleeing. I was rescuing myself from myself. I held the little bound bundle, and hurried home through the ever-more-humid night.

CHAPTER 8

. . . walk beside the child as she walks to the crater's mouth. The faeries say they must all jump in, that the volcano is a doorway into another world, the world in which the child's mother and father live, waiting for their child to return. The faeries say they found her as a baby on the lip of the volcano's mouth and res-cued her; they say they've been through the volcano many times. And when the girl jumps in the faeries jump with her, fall with her until the heat becomes too great, and then they unfold their wings, and the girl looks up at them as she falls, floating in the hot air. The faeries, given over to mirthful laughter in the least mirthful moments, don't laugh as they watch the girl fall. They did love her. They had taken care of her since she was a baby, since they had stolen her into the faerie world. The faeries had woven into her hair the petals of the flowers in which they nightly slept. They whispered to her secrets they didn't know they knew, deep secrets no one had told them—the holes in which the old gods slept in serpent shapes demanding sacrifice, the crushed root shaped into a baby that calmed the appetite of those vicious gods. They told her the most potent potion in the world could only be made from the venom of these snakes, but that no one had ever made it. It was a potion, the faeries told her, that brings the dead back to life. A dead flower touched with a drop will spring back to life, but it does not stay in full bloom; the petals close in on themselves and become a bud, and

the bud withdraws into the stem on which it heavily hung, the leaves infold themselves in themselves, and the writhing stem shrinks back into a tendril, and the tendril to a seed that waits in the ground for the warm sun to spring it. A drop of this potion brings back life, but life must start again from the beginning. The same happens to a man or woman on whom the potion is dropped. But the man becomes a boy, becomes a baby; the woman becomes a girl, becomes a baby. They remember nothing of their lives, save what appears to them in dreams. A child will sometimes dream of being in love before she knows what love is; she'll see a face in her dream and recognize it, a face she's never seen. It's all there, her whole life, the world of her life, beneath her memory. But the old life leaks through. The girl would listen to these stories the faeries told her and imagine that she had been a dead woman the faeries in their kindness had rescued. The faeries watched as the little girl they'd loved fell through the volcano and they could not laugh. The youngest of them (though faeries don't know their age, can't count years up, nor count numbers at all) cried just a few tears. A faerie's tears—so rarely do they ever occur—are a mortal danger to the faerie crying, for the tears are wrung from their essence. A faerie can die from crying. But one tear only dims its life briefly. That single tear is a strange and magical substance. It is heavy, heavier than all the faeries in the world put together (which would weigh nothing). The tear this faerie cried as she watched the little girl fall fell off her cheek and fell down faster than the girl was falling. The tear fell down through the volcano's heat and did not disappear. Just as the little girl was about to fall into the molten rock at the volcano's heart the *faerie's single tear fell on her. The tear fell into her open eye, and in an instant, she saw her whole life, saw herself being stolen from her house, saw herself in the leaf-boat on the magical river; she even saw her parents whose faces she could not before remember but now recognized and loved. She saw everything she had forgotten but which the faerie knew, for a tear is an intellectual thing, and to be cried for is to learn, to be cried for is to come to know. The faerie's tear fell into the little girl's eye and the little girl saw her own life. She plunged into the volcano's heart, into the burning lava, but she did not burn. She only kept falling through the furnace of the world, where rocks formed, where jewels were born. She saw creatures who labored in the fire that no human child had ever seen before. And then, the fire was gone, and she found herself sitting on the edge of a perfectly still pond on whose surface the sun brightly glowed. It was noon. The water was so bright it hurt to look at it. The girl's wet clothes were slowly drying in the sunlight. She stood up and thought about the faeries as a cloud covered the face of the sun and the pond reflected the cloud. She turned around and saw in the valley below her a house that she knew was her house. She know her mother and father waited inside as they had been waiting for so many years. And she decided it was time to walk home.*

I closed the book and put it on my bedside table. I pulled the chain that turned off the light. I closed my eyes in the dark.

✳

a man sitting by a circle but the circle is
a pond the man is sitting beside his head

is bent over and in
his lap is a book he bends over

crying as he reads what he reads looking
up saying lamentably "what shall

I do?" I am not there until he speaks
to me but he speaks and I am
there I am writing
a poem he says I am writing

a poem about a volcano it is a dream

already written the poem is

floating in the fire in the mouth

and the poet jumps into the mouth
the poet is the hero of this poem
but he burns up before he can read it

here I am writing my poem "what
shall I do?" he says lamentably he holds up

the page on which he's written one line

this is the only line I can write

on the page he's written one line

O O O O O O O O O

"you aren't here with me are you?" he says
"you're not even here with me I know I'm alone"

he bends his head over the page and cries

I know when I'm alone

✶

I was crying when I woke up. Early morning summer's light pale and blue. My pillow was a little wet.

I walked downstairs to my study; my father's study. I looked at the dark shadow on the bookshelf where the green book would be. Missing and found at the same time.

I took the pages out of the trash can. I shuffled them back into order, tapping the edges of the pages flush with each other. I wiped the dust off the top page. *An Impenetrable Screen of Purest Sky,* and below that in red ink my own name, and below my name line after line of blank musical staff, empty music beneath my name, empty breath waiting for a note.

The morning began when I cleared my throat and the hermit thrush sang.

CHAPTER 9

"Pearl?"

She looked up.

The voice in the air was her mother's voice, seeming as if it were spoken from a cloud. Pearl?—the voice from the cloud asked. And she answered—"Yes, I'm here."

Pearl's mother heard her daughter's voice spoken as if from under the bed, but it sounded quieter, as if it were coming from far away. Her mother looked under the bed, and saw the heating duct's hole. "Yes, I'm here" came out of the hole. Pearl's mother thought her daughter was caught in the bowels of the house, searching for the pearl she had lost. Her mother inched under the bed, inched herself to the hole, and, surprised at how wide it was, bent her body down in it. "Pearl?" "Yes, I'm here." And Pearl's mother dropped herself in to find her.

Her mother fell down the hole, but it was filled with water; she could breathe without breathing; she had no sense of panic. A picture in a frame fell through the water as an oak leaf falls off a tree, shuttling gently back and forth as it descended, a picture of a woman holding an umbrella, pink cheeks, looking gently down so that her eyes could not be seen; a picture of herself. There, open in the ocean, swaying in the current, was the blue umbrella she had tossed away after a violent gale destroyed its handmade spokes. A paper scroll rolled in waves within the waves. A white whale swam in a circle around her, swam between the objects floating in the sea; his tail knocked a blossom off an apple tree. The bottom of the ocean glowed brightly, a fact Pearl's mother found strange. She sank down toward the brightness as she watched a wedding dress—how could it be, but it was, her own—float up above her. Her head entered the brightness first, and she took a deep breath in the sun-filled air, felt sand under her feet, and walked up the shallows, the ocean wave silver at her heel, to shore.

"Pearl?"—she called out. "Pearl?—where are you?" "I'm here, Mother." And there she was, sitting with her back against a palm tree at the edge where beach turned to forest.

Pearl held a green book in her hand. "I knew you'd come," she said.

"I just read this story—" and Pearl held open a page on which an illustration showed a woman walking up from the ocean onto the beach, her arms held out, and a child standing up, waiting for her on the sand.

BOOK FOUR

FALL

CHAPTER 1

A CHILD'S FIRST EXPERIENCE OF THE WORLD IS NOT HIS *realization that adults are stronger but rather that he cannot make magic.* I read again this sentence that I had copied out many weeks before on a scrap of paper and left on my desk, weighted down by a stone against the open window's occasional breeze. I have spent many hours looking at it, pen in hand, nib unmoving on the page. Looked at it without comprehending it, seeing someone else's words in my own handwriting, as if the scrap weren't simply a reminder of a sentence that had sparked in me some dim recognition I wanted not to let go of, some thought in me silent and unknown, needing to be spoken by another to be perceived by me—those words written in my own hand like some mask worn inside the face instead of over it. Put on the mask of another's words and speak them as my own. *A child's first experience of the world* . . . is that he must make up a new language to speak about it, a magical language, in which every word creates the thing it names. Such a child might spend hours in his room, sitting in the dark closet, reciting words he made up and waiting to see if what he named appeared. This child might believe his words could change everything, that—just as asking in the night for a glass of water brought Father into his room

167

carrying a glass of cold water—so calling out into the closeted air secret names might bring forth greater miracles, darkest words attached to the deepest wishes, desires speakable only in this language that exists for no one but this child who, at times, maybe only once, yes, just once, spoke one word over and over again with such force he felt the closet walls shake around him, felt the ground he was sitting on tremble, felt it quake as if the floor were about to tear apart and open beneath him, not to swallow him but to let out those he called for, to return them to him, those whose secret name he finally had discovered after so many years of trying, of failing, of searching for the secret syllables in the songs of birds or in the furious buzz of a hummingbird's wings as it floats an instant before the flower before plunging itself in, and now he had found that word he knew existed, had heard it whispered in his ear when he found a nestling dead on the ground, this word he had spoken softly and then louder and louder until he felt his lungs ragged with the heat of yelling so that it could finally be heard; and when the ground did open there was no sound but only a blinding flash of light as he knew there would be, as he had expected but against which he could not keep his eyes open, and he felt as he knew he would arms around him, for he had called for these arms into the air; but then his eyes adjusted, and the arms around him weren't the right arms; they were his father's arms around him, holding him tightly against his own shaking to stop him shaking, pressing thumbs against his eyes to stop them crying, saying *calm, calm, it's* O.K., *calm, calm,* stroking his hair, soothing this boy whose open eyes seemed not to see anything, or to see everything at once, which is its own form of blindness; his father who picked him up in his arms, the strength of those arms against which the boy felt all his weight relax, his whole body in his father's arms. Such a child would, if there were such a child, if such a child had ever been . . .

There is, I thought, staring down still at the scrap, the terrible trouble of a life that is not your own. That's trouble enough. This always ever being oneself—myself. This endless self-taste that ends only when I end, as if my whole body were a tongue walking through the world, not just tasting what collided against it, but tasting itself taste, every sensation the inevitable proof of myself still being me. The classroom a stage in which I perform myself. The nagging rumor in dreams that every figure, not merely the younger self who wanders still through the mental woods watching the long-tailed blue birds snatch dragonflies from out the air, youth who looking down sees he's walking not through the fallen leaves of the deciduous trees but through the ash of the burnt forest, youth who wakes up as me to realize that even the ash is him, is myself.

It is the worm at the tongue's root—myself—that withers the words into dry silence when the topic shifts, when what asks for words is beyond me. Blank space of empty page, Sibyl's open hand—

My father returned but he never came home. There was a shipwreck in his face.

Grandma Clarel cried whenever she looked at him, and he asked her to leave. How old was I? I can't remember. I see myself sitting on her lap, my head buried in her shoulder, not crying, only breathing as gently as I could, as if I could learn to be so calm she would unknowingly carry me away with her, and I see myself as I am now, half-hearted professor, holding her hand at the kitchen table long after she has died, as if I had grown up at that table, had never left it, had never let her go, as if the kettle on the stove were just beginning to heat, and the water sounded like a tiny tympanum beat inside it, building to a crescendo that would never come.

But Grandma Clarel did leave. She bent down to me and said, "You have your mother's eyes." And then she hiccuped a small sob, stood up, met my father's gaze, who stood sallow and gaunt behind me, his hand on my shoulder as if I were the anchor holding him still, his hand clenched there like a hook, and said, "Allan, please ask me to come back if you need any help." I'd never heard her speak like that, with such precise tact. It made me cry to see how careful she was being; I felt that she was afraid for me. "We'll be fine, Clarel," my father said, not coldly, but with his now-continual lack of emotion. And as she stood on the porch, her giant portmanteau beside her, my father didn't turn around or turn me around, but, keeping his hand on my shoulder, pulled me backwards as he stepped into the house, keeping his eye on Grandma Clarel all the while, as if he were pulling me down into the darkness of the house as into a chasm, as if we were sinking and Grandma Clarel were the witness, and the door closing closed over us instead of in front of us.

I put the pen down. I read the scrap. I read the page I'd written.

Father never spoke about his journey. When he returned he no longer had the scroll. He never sat in his study at his desk singing out the strange words. He had killed the music in himself, or it had been killed. At night he would sometimes wake from terrible dreams, still asleep though his eyes were open. One night he stumbled hurriedly through the halls, his arms brushing the walls, chanting No, No, No, *over and over again, his penis hanging out of his pajama's fly, swinging back and forth as he jaggedly ran, and then, when he stopped running, when he stood still, when he stopped saying* No *and was silent, pointing obscenely at the ground.*

I read the page I'd written. I read the scrap. I put the pen down, thinking.

Safe, if slightly horrible, if somewhat weak, to write what I know. I have been witness to every page I've written, an open-eyed fact within the page and outside it, my being both character and writer at once. It is a simple drama that has no plot. Self gazing at self, dredging from dim memories crystalline moments—the angle of light on a pane of glass, the smell of sherry on breath—imagination wearing memory's mask to rescue clarity from dim suspicion. *I was, therefore I think.* But it's not enough. The endless detail of a half-forgotten day, details that could fill hundreds of pages and still describe nothing certainly, nothing actually—and why, now, do I see the pucker of Lydia's breast when she takes off her shirt in the early autumn chill . . . details to distract the mind from its own impotence. But life is elsewhere. Lurking at the boundary, where experience reaches its hazy edge across which it becomes something else, something known only by leaping into the unknown, where a monster sits, demonstrating patience. What must be said I will not say. I will not say because I cannot see. I need eyes that aren't my own. I need eyes that see by their own light. Imaginary eyes.

I looked at the scrap. I didn't read the page I'd written. I turned it over and put it on the pile. Beneath it another blank page marred by no word.

I looked at the pen. I picked up the scrap. I read it . . . *he cannot make magic*. I crumpled it up and threw it away.

I looked down at the blank page. The blank page is a form of light, lit by the eye as it tries to see itself see. The blank page is the eye's light.

CHAPTER 2

MEMORY CONJURES ABSENCE INTO PRESENCE. PAST scenes, none complete, fill the eye from behind— the eye also opens backward, pupil dilated wide in the mind's dark. Then the body moves by habit, the mind giving motion over to the muscles. I knew it was time to clean up the breakfast dishes and gather books and notes together and leave for school. I stood up from the chair and noticed, before my hand grabbed it, the dark crumbs of toast on the plate like stars across a porcelain sky—stars in reverse.

‡

Lydia put her clothes back on in the night. I watched her with some concern and some amusement from the bed, naked under the thin sheet. She buttoned her jeans, pulled her hair back and looped a band around it, and said, "Get dressed."

"Dressed? It's almost," looking at the clock's spectral numbers, "two in the morning. I'm just going to lay here in my state of blissful post-bliss and daze into unconsciousness."

"Nope. Not tonight, Lothario." She yanked the sheet off of me and I instinctively covered myself as if in sudden shame. She picked up my clothes from off the floor and threw them on the bed. "Tonight's the Perseids. We're going to go watch the sky fall down."

An autumn chill in the late August air—I remember it. Stars pricking through the old chaos. We lay with our backs on a hill. Lydia making order out of the disorder. Drawing the lines between the stars and telling me the names.

"It's beautiful, isn't it?"

I thought she was talking about the stars. "Yes," I said.

"All these points punctuating the sky against which we feel our smallness, this smallness we have always felt, this smallness." Her sentences seemed to run on in an ecstatic grammar. "And so people drew lines between the stars, found shapes and filled those shapes with stories." She sounded caught in reverie. "The stories mapped out the sky and explained it and then the reverse happened and the sky explained us. We named the stars and now they name us. Tell us the stories we've forgotten. It's beautiful. It *is* beautiful. Against all the nothingness we have always felt we fill in the tales that add up to . . . something, to somethingness. And these stars, they mark their flat shape in the sky only because the eye can't see their depth. The stars so infinitely away from each other, so that the lines that tell the stories reach back across light years and knot together onto one page wholly different books of time and distance. They knot together different worlds. The sky is—it's this novel above us. All written on a single page. It's this poem. There's Lyra"—pointing up at a group of stars I could not honestly discern, moving her arm in a diamond shape that mimicked the constellation—"Orpheus's lyre."

I gazed in the direction she pointed. Shapeless cluster of light. "Orpheus saw Tantalus in the underworld. Standing in a flood but no drop would enter his mouth to drink. An apple near his lip that would always withdraw. Orpheus saw him, and he played a song on his lyre that stilled the water and apple, and Tantalus drank and ate."

"Of course he did." She placed my hand underneath her shirt. The warmth of her belly. I moved my hand down under the waistband of her underwear where the first curled strands of hair marked the intimate geography. She ran her hand carelessly up and down my arm. "Desire and song. Song and desire," she said it as if she were reciting the primal elements, invoking the oldest gods.

Then Lydia leaned up quickly on her elbow and pointed up. "Look!"

And a dozen green fuses lit themselves in the sky and fell through the lyre, striking the strings whose music we could see but could not hear.

✱

Clink of plate in porcelain sink. Shush of water rinsing off crumbs.

✱

Walking in the October night. Windy but sparse clouds. The leaves blowing across the ground.

"Do you remember your mother at all?" Lydia asked.

A gust blew leaves against my legs, and then died, covering the path. "There's only one memory that feels certain." The image filled my eye. "I remember being in the kitchen. My mother's back was to me. She was doing the dishes. I don't remember her face. I only remember her taking both hands out of the sink and flicking the water off of them—but the motion was strange, she moved both hands in the same direction, at the same time, a rhythm or a dance, or as if she were signaling something coming toward her to move over so they wouldn't collide." Another gust cleared the path. I could hear the leaves rolling away on their thin, dead edges. "I don't remember her face. My grandma used to tell me I had her eyes. I would sometimes stare at my face in the mirror and try to find her in it. But I only remember her flicking the water off her hands, a memory that keeps repeating in my mind when I remember it, as if she's going to do it forever."

Lydia took my hand.

"Those three stars," pointing. "Do you see them?"

I looked up where she was pointing and saw dozens, some so faint I wasn't sure I was seeing them at all. "Yes," I said.

"Those will be ours." She spoke as if she had finally found the answer to a question that had long been troubling her. "That's our constellation. It marks our story."

✳

Wandered through the rooms gathering what I needed for the day. Flicking off the kitchen light. Stepping unconsciously over the creaky board in the old floor.

In the old world, in the ancient world, when people died they knew they were in the underworld because they found themselves repeating the same gesture over and over again: running water through a sieve, rolling a rock uphill, flicking from fingers the soapy water.

I gathered what I needed. Flicked off the kitchen light. Stepped over the creaky board in the old floor.

I gathered what I needed. Flicked off the lights. Stepped over the creaky board.

I went to my office to get my books.

I went to my office to get my books.

✻

My father leaned against the window repeating what sounded like *and* over and over again, each time in a lower tone, until the word felt like a pressure in the air vibrating in the ear, and then the window began to rattle, louder and louder, the one loose pane buzzing as loudly as a bee in a flower, louder, a bee mistaking an ear for a flower, and gathering within it all the heard words for its pollen, only to fly back and feed the hive on song; and then the buzzing ceases, but even in silence seems to continue—not a sound but a motion, almost atomic—and Father turned around to see me, and the way he looked at me, as if I were an entire world still undiscovered.

✳

Picking up my pen from the desk. Silver poplar yellowing outside the window.

✳

My father leaned against the window whispering to himself his wife's name, *Maria, Maria, Maria,* each time more quietly, until only breath. Then even breath was silence.

He turned around to see me, and the look in his face, in his eyes, as if I were a world lost to him forever.

✳

Wandered through the house to find what I'd forgotten. What I'd forgotten stayed forgotten. I never could find it as I walked back through. I always had the feeling something was missing, but nothing was ever missing. I stood by the dining room table, tips of fingers of both hands tense against it, eyes closed, as if channeling spirits, as if leading a séance at which no one else arrived.

✳

Lydia at night at the dining room table, papers and books spread around her. She leaned her face against one hand and—as if the other hand did not belong to her—watching as her pencil marked the circumference of a circle over and over again, never following the line perfectly, so that the first definite edge grew blurrier, more complex, as if the orbit were wobbling.

I saw that the floor was littered with dozens of such pages.

She didn't look at me as she spoke. "It's a terrible knot."

"What is?"

"All of it is a terrible knot."

"You'll untie it," I said.

She laid her pencil down on the page. "No," she said, "the secret isn't to solve it. The secret is to pull it tighter."

✳

Picking up the keys from the glass dish, cheap trinket won years ago, seaside town at dusk, houses' windows lit up yellow but printed so poorly on the glass the little yellow squares were off-center, and the yellow light seemed to be burning gently through the inside of all the houses in town. The mistaken stars stamped in the sky. Picking up the keys, picking up the spare change.

✳

For many years, after Lydia left me, for many years, always in March, a postcard would arrive in the mail. The pictures on the postcards stick in my mind: a pond the small type on the underside says is Walden Pond, a hummingbird in front of a flower, a page from the first edition of Emerson's essay—in which underlined in red ink (and this pressed into the card, marked by the sender) *We would look about us, but with grand politeness he draws down before us an impenetrable screen of purest sky, and another behind us of purest sky. "You will not remember," he seems to say, "and you will not expect."*—, Greek vase on which Hermes forever is stealing Apollo's sacred cattle, a violin in a glass case, a handmade butterfly made of gold, a lithograph of a whaling ship with a whale breaching over it, Pan playing the flute, and an antique mirror in whose convex surface no one appeared. For nine years a postcard would arrive, this was always in March. Nothing was written on them save my address in a nondescript, blocky hand. But pressed into each one were three marks, three stars, handwritten asterisks, in the same configuration each time.

Every year, in March, someone sent me a constellation. The constellation was mine. The card I knew came from Lydia.

And then, one year, the postcards stopped.

Sometimes at night I would walk outside to try and find those stars. But the night was a book I could not read. There was no one to translate the stars. One of those stories was my story, but I didn't know which one. My story was above me, not mine. I looked up and the light-pierced dark unscrolled dumb always above dumb me.

✻

The door closed behind me.

　　I mean to say, I closed the door behind me.

　　I closed the door behind me, and I left.

CHAPTER 3

Sometimes I thought I could hear it, the earth rolling in its rut. But it was always just the wind crushing the leaves—I mean, blowing through them.

It was a windy day.

Sometimes I thought I could see it, the wind blowing over the land, the ferocious body of the wind larger than the earth it shook.

But it wasn't the earth that was shaking.

But it wasn't the wind I could see.

I found a note taped to my office door. *Stopped by to discuss paper. See you in class. Ishmael.* I'd forgotten we'd made an appointment. I opened the door, peeled off the note. Ishmael's handwriting looked strangely elongated, letters distended as if stretched past the limit of their elasticity. His script was like he was, trying to express more than the limit could hold. In class he seemed at times painfully inward, each sentence spoken by another student a blow that bruised him. Other times he spoke with an eloquence that seemed to surprise him, almost to control him, a brilliance he could not reconstruct later without the leaping antilogic of intuitive realization. We would often talk after class, walking down the hall together. Ishmael stepped very lightly—when he was silent it was if he wasn't there beside me, there and not there at the same time. He'd sit down in the chair across from me, gaze distractedly out the window, glance at the titles of books on the shelves, look at the floor, as if by looking from side to side he could find a way to reconstruct those thoughts in full whose vestiges glittered in his mind. He would at such times have the ravaged look of a man less complete than the ideas he contained—a look not quite of despair, but of a certain kind of helplessness made palpable only by virtue of the inaccessible secret, a kind of power, whose intricate knot kept tying itself tighter within him; one that he could witness, feel within him, but that he could not untie himself. He was a strange boy, a wonderful one; in some ways, I felt I loved him, a feeling that frightened me, that made me frightened of him. I folded the note up along the crease he'd pressed into it, and then folded it in half again, and then again, until it could no longer be folded, and, half-mindedly, slipped it in my pocket.

A novel, I thought, even a short story—taking books and notes out of my bag and placing them neatly on my desk—fills itself with sentences that do the mundane work. *I walked down the hallway* because a character I call "I" must walk down the hallway to get to a room where something must occur or be found; *I poured myself a cup of coffee and walked down the hall to the study.* Setting the scene, adding a detail— *the spring night was cold; a flash of sunlight on leaf.* These sentences that trigger the imagination's base, unspoken-of need for logic, for the everyday;

these sentences that contain no thought, no realization, that move the reader's mind down the hall with a hot cup of coffee warming his or her hand, this trick of words that conjures memory in the nerves, thoughtless sentences whose only effort is to make what does not exist seem actual. It leaves, I thought, noticing four dead flies on the windowsill and brushing them into my hand, a bad taste in my mouth. I threw the flies away. The air of the room had a scent I had never noticed before, and if the odor was new or if I hadn't in all the years I've worked in this office been sensitive enough to discern it, I couldn't say; it smelled like an old book just opened. Absurdly, the image came to mind of the whole of Trillbyrne Hall being one page in a giant pop-up book, and as I puttered around my office, arranging my books, arranging my notes, looking out the window in my continual abstraction—I mean distraction—I did so only because a child somewhere past the horizon of my meager realization pulled the paper tab with the arrow pointing down. I wish there were a way to put my thoughts away. But that is the nature of distraction—and distracted is what I am—that it teaches thought to evade capture by flinging it always into the speed of its own momentum. In the middle of one pane of glass I saw a handprint that must be my own. Seeing it stopped my mind's wandering. I thought, *There's work to do.* I thought, *I'm at work.*

The edition of Hawthorne's stories I had ordered for class contained in it mistakes I found wonderful even as my students complained in frustration. One signature of pages had been sewn in backwards and upside down, so that in the middle of "Young Goodman Brown," as he's walking through the dark woods, the students found themselves, at page's turn, staring at the last sentence of "Rappaccini's Daughter," *Just at that moment, Professor Pietro Baglioni looked forth from the window, and called loudly, in a tone of triumph mixed with horror, to the thunder-stricken man of science: "Rappaccini! Rappaccini! And is* this *the upshot of your experiment?"* printed upside down on the bottom of the page, a number hanging dizzyingly above it on the topmost margin like four apples—*88*—about to fall off an invisible tree. It was also missing the last page of the story we were to have read for today, "The Artist of the Beautiful." I picked up my old copy and walked down the hallway to the photocopier. Passing Olin's office I noticed the door slightly ajar, so I pushed it open to say hello. I saw, though so quickly I couldn't be sure I did see, Olin's hand on a student's knee; but when the door fully opened, when my own shape filled the frame, Olin was leaning back in his chair, arms crossed over the slight paunch of his stomach, looking as nonplussed as ever.

"Hello, Daniel."

"Olin," I said, returning the mock cordiality of his tone.

The young man whose back was to me reached down and grabbed the strap of his backpack. He stood up, the bag so heavy with books he tilted back down. "Thank you, Professor," he said. He turned quickly around, eyes cast downward, cheek burning, saying "excuse me" with quick politeness as I moved to the side to let him leave the room.

"Call me Olin. Why rest on formality?" Olin called after him as he left. "Youth," Olin said. "Innocence." He said these words as if they could not exist together for long.

"Olin—" I said his name with the slightest hint of recrimination at which he opened his eyes wide in childish awe.

"Daniel—" he said in the same way.

And suddenly, frustrated by the game, "Have a good class," and I turned around and left.

Olin called out after me, "A drink later?" When I turned around he was leaning out into the hallway, one hand clenching the doorframe, the other hand waving at me as I walked away.

"Yes. A drink."

I held the book down against the glass as the green light's line scanned forward and backward. The same page spat out eighteen times in the tray. I picked them up, turned them over, only to find that beneath the reproduced page from the book the bottom of my palm appeared, jagged crosshatched lines dark against the pressed skin's white pad. I looked at my palm, loose paper clasped inside the book in my other hand. Thick line below my little finger that bent upward toward my index finger as it tapered into nothing; thicker line beginning below my index finger that breaks into two lines as a river breaks, one stream trickling into nothing in the middle of my hand, and the other, a semicircle skirting the hill at the base of the thumb. (The mind finds a landscape and makes a map; sometimes it sees a landscape that is not there.) A thin line, a spicule line, that cut across the middle of my hand, dividing one line in two, nearing the curving line next to the thumb but never touching it, as if in my hand were a child's math lesson, a graph showing how a curving line never touches the other, how between those two lines there is always a gap, even if the gap is infinitesimal. Simple geometries etched in the hand, and impossible ones. The hand contains its own parable. It bears on it lines of trajectory that cross, shows points of intersection; and later it reveals that what collides never touches; it bears, as if burned into it at birth, a chart of the *innavigable sea* between us and all things.

"What is it, Daniel? New love? Old love? Fear death by water? Riches? Poverty? A new career? Fame after death? What do you see? What's the future?" Olin stood outside the door in the hall, bemused.

"Poverty then riches," I said. "Class then drink." I put my hand in my pocket and felt the folded note at the bottom of it. "I'll see you at three."

I walked down the hall, back to my office. A scent in the air as of an old book opened for the first time in a century.

I wondered how the book I carried in my hand stayed in my hand; I wondered how it didn't fall.

CHAPTER 4

I WALKED INTO THE CLASSROOM LATE AND CLOSED THE door behind me. A young woman bent down to take her book from her bag, and as she did so, her blouse fell away from her chest revealing a nipple's dark edge. She sat back up, looked at me, and said "Hello, Professor." She didn't blush; nor did I.

I walked to the front of the class and sat down at the desk. I put the book and papers on it. The class sat before me, all in their orderly rows.

"What is that?" I asked, noticing something small on the floor near Ishmael's foot. "That, right there," I asked, pointing.

Ishmael looked on either side of him, and the young woman sitting next to him, the woman whose breast I had just seen, bent over to pick it up. Ishmael watched her as she leaned over and down, then looked suddenly away, embarrassed. She stood up and walked to the desk, her hand held out in front of her; she seemed to me to move slowly, her arm outstretched almost as if in a trance, an initiate into the mysteries, or the one who has decided to initiate me. "Here you are." She held her hand out palm-side down, so that I had to cup my hand beneath hers, and then in a sudden motion she released all her fingers at once, as if flicking a drop of water from the tip of each one; I felt the tiny object drop into my hand, warmed by the warmth of her skin. She took two steps backwards still facing me, turned gently around by pivoting on one foot—as if within the mundane time of class and day she had found (we all had unwittingly found ourselves in) some other time, some Arcadian zone that hides itself within the passing minutes of taking attendance and going over the details of the next assignment, some ancient time unpassing within passing time, time that exists but cannot be spoken of, cannot be sensed or claimed, lest at the point of recognition it disappear again, timelessness being casualty to consciousness—walked back to her desk and sat down. I looked down in my hand. Sitting in the crease of a line in my palm was a pearl. I picked it up and held it between two fingers. I felt speechless. I looked out at the class; I looked out at the class with my blank face. "How?—"

"An earring?" Ishmael offered.

"Maybe a ring, a loose setting?" said the woman who had picked it up.

Hearing such rational explanations comforted me. An instant before, the world felt too unreal, or more than real—the appearance of a pearl on the floor of my class an event of almost cosmic bewilderment, as astonishing as a new star appearing in the sky where none had been before, something inexplicable, some brittle line shattered, some edge crossed or fallen over, something rent in the air, making the old world only a nostalgia of what used to be, and offering this new one, where pearls leaped into existence out of nothingness, falling through a hole in the air. "Of course. Right. A ring or an earring; an earring or a ring. That makes perfect sense." I said it as if the phrase were a little song. The class laughed uncomfortably. I stood up and put the pearl in my pocket. I grabbed the pile of pages. "You might have noticed an omission in our none-too-carefully crafted book. A missing last page, for example." I paused, waiting for the class to gripe, but no one complained. "Well, to end the awful suspense, I made copies of the missing page." I handed the pile to the student sitting closest to me, and watched as it diminished page by page as it wound its way through the class. When everyone had one, I sat back down, opened my book to the page they all held in their hands, and began to read:

As if the butterfly, like the artist, were conscious of something not entirely congenial in the child's nature, it alternately sparkled and grew dim. At length it arose from the small hand of the infant with an airy motion that seemed to bear it upward without an effort, as if the ethereal instincts with which its master's spirit had endowed it impelled this fair vision involuntarily to a higher sphere. Had there been no obstruction, it might have soared into the sky and grown immortal. But its lustre gleamed upon the ceiling; the exquisite texture of its wings brushed against that earthly medium; and a sparkle or two, as of stardust, floated downward and lay glimmering on the carpet. Then the butterfly came fluttering down, and, instead of returning to the infant, was apparently attracted toward the artist's hand.

"Not so! not so!" murmured Owen Warland, as if his handiwork could have understood him. "Thou has gone forth out of thy master's heart. There is no return for thee."

With a wavering movement, and emitting a tremulous radiance, the butterfly struggled, as it were, toward the infant, and was about to alight upon his finger; but while it still hovered in the air, the little child of strength, with his grandsire's sharp and shrewd expression in his face, made a snatch at the marvellous insect and compressed it in his hand. Annie screamed. Old Peter Hovenden burst into a cold and scornful laugh. The blacksmith, by main force, unclosed the infant's hand, and found within the palm a small heap of glittering fragments, whence the mystery of beauty had fled forever. And as for Owen Warland, he looked placidly at what seemed the ruin of his life's labor, and which was yet no ruin. He had caught a far other butterfly than this. When the artist rose high enough to achieve the beautiful, the symbol by which he made it perceptible to mortal senses became of little value in his eyes while his spirit possessed itself in the enjoyment of the reality.

As I read I found myself taking the pearl out of my pocket, rubbing it between thumb and fingers. An unconscious motion that mimicked the work of the mind, rolling the object of contemplation around, touching it, to find out what it might be. It was not the pearl that was the mind.

I looked up at the class. A few students were furiously writing in their notebooks. Others gazed down at the floor, or over at the wall, or their eyes kept to one corner unseeing, vision now an internal sense as they pictured the golden gears and golden dust in the baby's open hand destroyed. Ishmael looked out the window. He looked upset.

I stood up and walked to the front of my desk, and leaned back against it. "Well, someone, tell me what you think."

I like a silence that thinks itself, this silence of the class listening to itself, to the words no one yet is speaking but which many are sensing, almost hearing, fate or future, the conversation to come.

"I didn't expect it," a voice called out. I didn't see who spoke.

"Why not?" I asked. "Owen's work had been destroyed before, although in earlier stages. Destroyed by Peter Hovenden's doubt, destroyed by Annie's—this woman Owen loved—not understanding his work, the audacity and beauty of his endeavor." A hand raised. "Yes, Lisa?"

"But this time it's different. Before he hadn't done it. Hadn't built it." The metallic screech of a bluejay's call outside the window echoed in the room as if offering itself as a clue. "Now it seems his life's work is worthless. He's a . . ." she hesitated to say it, "a failure."

"How can you say that?" Ishmael said, turning on her, as if he was the one who had been insulted. "He's not a failure. He's an artist. He's the artist of the beautiful, and it doesn't matter that the butterfly was destroyed. It's better. It should have been destroyed."

Lisa looked shocked but didn't retreat. "Why? You think there's something noble in destruction. But there's not. You think destruction is creative, some writing class nonsense. You think you're being an idealist, an artist yourself, but really you're just speaking out of fear—that nothing beautiful can last."

"Nothing beautiful does last." Ishmael pronounced it like a verdict. "What's beautiful isn't beautiful because it exists, because it can fill the hand. It's not beautiful because it can be seen or held. It's beautiful in some other way. Its beauty means something else, something better. It's just an object—"

"But that object was his life's work. The object was a work of art," a student from the back of the room spoke up. "Everything he'd learned and taught himself for his whole life was in that butterfly. The baby destroying it—it's like the baby crushed Owen in his hand, too."

I kept rolling the pearl between fingers, looking down at it. "Then why wasn't Owen upset? The butterfly acted as if it wanted to fly back to the hand, and so to the safety, of the man who made it. But Owen refuses it, forces it to fly back to the child. Why?"

Ishmael spoke immediately. "Because it's no longer his."

"Why?"

"Because what you make doesn't belong to you. Not if you're an artist. Because art is always a gift. It's always given. It's not a selfish work. It's—," and here he paused, as if overcome with emotion, "always an act of love."

Lisa spoke, catching the glimmer of the thought. "And the child, the baby—it's also an act of love. I mean, the baby comes out of love, the act of love." She blushed deeply red as if she had just spoken obscenely.

"So the child and the butterfly are the same, or similar—" I said.

"—and different," Ishmael added in a hushed voice. "The child's not a work of art. He's a work of the body. The butterfly is a work of art."

"But Owen must build it. It does exist materially," I said. "It is an object. If it weren't a body, even if a mechanical body, it couldn't be destroyed." I closed my hand around the pearl. "But it feels to me that you're both right. The baby and Owen's butterfly are the same and different, a one and a many. Form is the beginning of mortality. Annie herself says that the infant seems to 'know more of the mystery than we do.'" It as if the child and the butterfly have both come into the world from some shared place, some fecund nothingness or creative chaos that doesn't exactly exist but makes existence possible. Some people call it soul, or spirit, or pneuma—some call it breath. The butterfly is powered by perpetual motion, this was Owen's great discovery that Peter Hovenden so skeptically dismissed—the perpetual motion. Its artistry is that Owen had found a way to fuse soul to matter, to animate gold and gears and even dust into a harmony of impossible flight. The child, too, is the same impossibility. The heart beats and it's not simply an electrical pulse, it's not only the nerves. The child is closer to the mystery the butterfly is manifest proof of—that something is pulled from some other region, some other realm or world, Eros and Chaos, Memory and Power, Mother and Father, formlessness and form, something no word does justice to, something a word in trying to name dispels, this mystery in life that life can be." I opened my hand and looked at the pearl. I held it up in front of my eye, pinched between thumb and finger. "Sometimes I wonder how much of what is real is a choice we make. We make this choice every day, every minute—maybe we are right now choosing if this instant is real, this conversation. For some of you it will be, and for others of you, it will simply be something less than experience, an hour time moved through with you as its distracted witness." I pinched the pearl harder; I could feel its surface pressing into my skin. "For Annie, that reality is the body, the body of her child, that body made in love and pleasure with her husband, the body that feeds off her body, which suckles life from her breast." I pinched the pearl so hard it shot from my fingers, hit the ground with a small and hollow knock and rolled down the aisle in a straight line—it sounded like a pencil drawing a line on a page—toward Ishmael, who bent down, cupped his hand over it, and picked it up. "And the butterfly takes life from somewhere else. Maybe Owen's soul. Maybe the soul that if it is eternal is also infinite and so exists, if it exists, not within us but outside us . . . maybe art is that creation which puts on form as a soul puts on a body, but doesn't privilege the body, doesn't revel in the form, but waits again to be released to be realized, for what is real, what is chosen as what is real, isn't the gold flakes, isn't the gold gears, isn't the golden glow of those handmade wings. What's real is the force that through the wings makes the butterfly fly. It is just as real when the butterfly is destroyed. Maybe it's more real then. It's just as real when the body is dead."

As soon as I said that last word, *dead,* Ishmael stood up and left the room.

I followed him out, called after him down the hall. He paused and I caught up to him. "What's wrong?"

He turned around. He was crying. "I'm sorry," he said. "I remembered my mother. Something about that conversation made me remember my mother."

"You miss her?"

"Yes, I miss her." He looked at me. "She died when I was ten."

I walked back to class. The students were sitting quietly, an uncomfortable quiet.

"Your papers are due on Monday," I said. "Please find me if you have any concerns or questions." Everyone made their way, one by one, out of the room.

On Ishmael's desk, in the very center of his desk, with its strange luster, with its strange glow, was the pearl.

✳

Olin was perched on a stool at the bar when I walked in, and seeing me, he stood up, a beer in each hand, and walked over. "Daniel," he said, "you arrive and I'm pre-pared." He handed me my pint, put his hand on my shoulder, and guided me back to our favorite booth. The jukebox played continuously the blues with which the owner had filled it; he had covered up the coin slot with a piece of black electric tape. The old 78s spread out fan-like behind the glass. Robert Johnson in the air, *the blue light was my baby, and the red light was my mind,* and Olin unconsciously humming the tune.

"So, how's it going?"

"What?" I asked.

"It," Olin said in a tone of mock doom.

"The novel?"

"It," in the same voice, "yes, it."

"I wake up and work on it pretty much every day. And every day I think about throwing it back in the trash." I took a sip of beer. "The trouble is my father."

"Fathers are always the trouble, Daniel. Isn't that true?"

"The trouble is I can't see through his eyes. The trouble is imagination. The trouble is me being me trying to be someone else, someone I knew but didn't know, the trouble is—well, the whole thing is the trouble. Me being me. That trouble."

"Throw it out. Work on something sensible."

"That might be the first time you've ever given me good advice, Olin."

"Well, I was trying to tell a joke. Couldn't you hear the sarcasm?"

"It's so much your general tone I think I missed it."

"You're afraid to imagine, Daniel. I've always known this about you. Not that you idolize facts. You're no material zealot. You're no *proofist*—that's what I call them. You're something else. Devoted to a god you won't let yourself believe in. The novel is a half-formed worship, the novice practicing and practicing because he's afraid to stop practicing and commit." Olin had never spoken to me in actual judgment before. I felt taken aback. I drank more beer and looked aside. "Your father—"

"What do you know about my father? Why are you even talking about him?"

"I know what you've told me."

"And that's it—that's nothing. My father—he—"

"Yes?"

I took another gulp of beer. I looked at Olin. "I don't know what to say next. I don't know what the next words are." The next record mechanically slipped onto the player. *I don't know why I love you like I do, stormy weather* . . . "It's a blank page."

"I'm sorry, Daniel. I didn't mean to upset you."

"Please, don't worry. It's me, actually. I feel very on edge." I picked up my beer surprised to find it was already empty. "Do you know a student named Ishmael?" I asked.

"No. And a name I would have remembered, I suspect."

"He's in my class. We've become close."

"That's good. Isn't it?" Olin's persona had been stripped of its delight in innuendo.

"Good? I suppose. I don't know. I feel—" I paused, not knowing how to admit to someone else what I could hardly admit to myself. "I think that I might be his father."

Olin stared at me, eyes growing wider, slightly watering as if he were to break into tears, as if he were affected by the thought as much as I was, as if tears were the only appropriate response to something so impossible, so unimaginable; and then he broke into an uproar of laughter so violent he kept hitting his fist against the table, the candle's flame guttering inside its glass. "You kill me, Daniel. You really do. You kill me."

CHAPTER 5

PEARL AND HER MOTHER SAT ON THE SHORE, LOOKING out at the ocean where the white whale breached, drops of water sparkling in the sunlight, and looking down at the pages of the book. "It's our story," Pearl said, turning a few pages back to show her mother an illustration where a young girl stole a black box off a dresser drawer's top. She turned the page and her mother read *The girl meant to catch it, but didn't. It hit the side of her hand and bounced away, fell onto the ground, and rolled across the floor with a noise that sounded like a pencil drawing a dark line on a page* . . . but Pearl turned the page again before she could finish the sentence. Every time a page turned her mother thought the sky above them turned suddenly but briefly darker, as if a cloud had passed across the face of the sun—but there were no clouds in the sky. "And look," Pearl said, turning a few more pages, "here we are." And there sat Pearl and her mother together on the beach, heads bent down over a book. Her mother took the book from Pearl, and began turning over page after page, looking for where the story ended. A last page showed them on hands and knees, peering down into a pond, their reflections marked in a thin and shaky line.

Pearl's mother took her by the hand, pulled her to her feet, and they walked together into the forest that edged the shore as far as they could see. There was no path, but they had no difficulty finding their way; not scared by Pearl and her mother, the birds kept singing. Pearl said, "And Mother, do you know, there are so many other stories in the book I looked at while I was waiting for you—a story about a girl who grew up with the faeries and they tricked her into jumping into a volcano, and—" A hummingbird whose long tail feathers curled into scrolls floated for an instant before them as if wondering what flowers were these that moved as they blossomed, and unable to solve the mystery, flew off and disappeared into a large bell-shaped flower.

"And Mother, there's a story, I saw the pictures, of a man on a sea voyage, and he stands at the front of the ship in a raging storm and his mouth is open like he's singing, and—" Her mother pulled two fruit from a low-hanging branch, and she and Pearl ate the fruit.

Then the thick woods began to clear. Then they stepped into the clearing.

There—shining water—was a pond.

✳

Pearl and her mother walked to the edge of the pond.

Water bubbled in the middle, fed by a spring below. "Hello," a voice said.

Pearl and her mother saw a man sitting near the water on the opposite side of the pond, sitting with his knees bent, a book propped up on his knees, a pen in his hand. "Hello," Pearl said, "Who are you?" "I am writing a poem about a volcano," the man said, as if who he was were what he was doing. "I'll read it to you, if you want," the man said, "O O O O O O O O O."

"That man's not in the picture in the book," Pearl whispered to her mother. Her mother only held Pearl's hand tighter, and they walked to the edge of the pond. They knelt down and peered into the water; they stared through their own faces staring back up at them. But beneath their faces, looking through the looking of their own eyes, Pearl and her mother began to see some-thing—not simply the pond's fine silt bottom, but some-thing below the silt, an image coming into form, as through a dust-coated window a dim figure outside can be seen approaching. "Look, Mother, look down there," Pearl said, "it's a room, a schoolroom—Mother, look." Her mother did look; she saw the room, too—the vision becoming clearer and clearer, the blur resolving into forms forming into students walking out of the room. Then only one man was left, his face unseen, though Pearl's mother felt she must know him, this stranger whose posture to her seemed familiar, as if she had known him in a life she had forgotten almost com-pletely, so familiar her heart beat not faster but deeper, drumming in her chest. "Mother, Mother, look!—there it is, there is your pearl!—" and her mother saw it, too, a single pearl in the middle of a desk in the middle of a schoolroom and one man, head bent down, looking at it. Pearl put her hand in the water, as if to retrieve the pearl, to return it to her mother, but the water parted around her hand, the water rippled, and the world beneath the surface disappeared, leaving Pearl and her mother again staring only at themselves, and then the surface grew agitated, the ripples grew into larger waves, and as they watched, the waves erased their faces, leaving only their eyes, and then the water closed their eyes, the water closed their eyes, and sitting up, all there was to see was each other.

CHAPTER 6

I STEPPED ON THE LETTERS WHEN I OPENED THE DOOR. I picked them up, shuffled through them one by one, seeing my own name printed over and over again distinguished only by different fonts. It is reading one's name that gives one the feeling of being anonymous, I thought, peering at my name beneath the cellophane window of a phone bill, placing it behind the pile I'd already glanced through, when behind it I found a picture, a postcard, and reproduced on it—though a poor reproduction where colors bled outside of their form, a neon green edge to the woman's blue sleeve looking almost like an aura—was Gustave Moreau's *Orpheus*. A woman holds Orpheus's severed head and gazes down at it, save her eyes are closed. She stares at him through her closed eyes, which is how one sees memory. His eyes too are closed, which is how one sees when one is dead. They look at each other through closed eyes. The edge of the postcard was ragged, torn, as if it had been caught in between the teeth of two gears. I turned it over. A note taped to the back said, *This postcard got caught in a sorting machine and fell behind it. We found it while making repairs, and so are delivering it now. We apologize for the inconvenience.* I peeled the note off, transparent tape pulling up the thick paper's fibers. I had the sudden sensation of

204

peeling a bandage off a wound. Underneath the note, pressed deep into the paper in blue ballpoint, three stars darkly shined. I recognized them. They were mine. After so many years, years in which I thought Lydia had finally decided to forget me, worse years where I felt something worse happened, that she had gotten sick, been hurt; worse today when in the hall the boy I thought might be my son told me his mother had died long ago and walked away from me in tears. But she wasn't dead. But I wasn't forgotten. We still stared—across the entire distance—at each other, eyes not closed but open. The postcard had no words, only this constellation that told me again my own story, this story written above me in the stars, the stars Lydia named, and written down on the cream-colored sky of this card in dark blue ink, a note to say that in this world there exists this woman I loved, whom I love still, whom I failed, whom I sent away, who knows where in the vast sky to look up and find those three points of light that mark no others but us, those stars whose story we are. My hand shook. The stars shook in my hand. And then I glanced at the postmark's smudged red ink, *March 10,* but the year was smeared almost past recognition, so that I brought the card closer to my face, turned it from side to side to see if I could make out the impression of the numbers pressed into it, rubbed my finger over the surface, and then I saw it, or sensed it, not that I could make out the year in any undeniable way, but that my doubt grew definitive, made my senses more keen, proved to me exactly what I refused to believe—the year read *19*—, eight years ago. I looked back over my shoulder, but no one was behind me. No one was behind me at all. And when I looked back at the card the stars seemed to me eyes that were closed, and that Lydia was peering at me through eyes she had borrowed, eyes that saw in delay, the eyes of the disappeared, just as the stars still seem to send out their light long after the spark that throws it has died.

The light on in the hallway shone bright enough through the open door to let me see the words on the page as I wrote them. I tried to never work at night, when my day-dulled mind sensed less, dimmed by the hours' intravenous opiate. I looked at the postcard on my desk, propped up against a paperweight, at the three stars scratched into it. It wasn't memory. It wasn't memory I had to write. It was memory's opposite, which the day's forgetfulness alone makes possible to see. I picked up my pen. I turned over the last written page. There it was. And it was blank.

He watched the ship move away to the horizon, and when at the horizon, he watched it disappear. He stood on the rocks and hummed to himself and he watched the ship turn into nothing. He thought he had also disappeared to them. He had become a single point, anonymous, fated only to begin a line and end a line and travel the circuit between. Here I am, he thought—this man who had ceased to think of himself as someone who says "I," this man who felt he was narrating his own story even as he lived it, this man who thought of himself as "he," and in stranger moments, stronger moments, thought of himself below any name that hints at the human, "it," and in exalted real-ization, "a"—a singer standing on the singing rocks. For it was as he had read, and in dreams as he had seen, names scratched into platelike rocks, livid white letters against the stone's deep gray, the only record of the lives those names named, lost even now at sea, floating forever to the ocean's bed, the white whale swimming in delight or in blindness among them, judging and forgiving, ignoring and abandoning. These names were their graves. Allan, *he said out loud.* Allan, *he said again, pressing his tongue against the back of his teeth, extending the last let-ter's sound—nnnnnn—until it rang in the ear, as if testing the one thing he still knew about himself, that the letter at the end of his name was a secret bell he spent his life learning to ring. He had come to find out what door it is that bell asks to open. He took the scroll from his bag and held it tightly in his hand, and then began to make his way over the rocks to the path, a dull ringing music marking every step, a music that died quickly, the music of the names of the lost.*

Certain experiences precede themselves, and the supersti-tious call this déjà vu. But he wasn't superstitious. He knew how words work when sung. When sung a word uses what it names as an arrow uses a bow, and where that arrow lands is where experience opens, long in advance of the archer's foot find-ing the quiver still vibrating in the ground. This is Apollo's les-son—archer god of poetry and vision. The lyre is also a bow. The poet also a hunter. But the poet is a hunter in reverse; the poet is that hero who hunts the dead so as to return them to life. He is a poet, Allan thought about himself.

He walked along the path, lighter rocks in a line between the darker ones. The landscape looked covered in cinders, not ash—half-burnt and only waiting a spark hot enough to finish the conflagration. The largest boulders moved—those ancient tortoises whose shells scraped against the ground, grinding rock against rock, forever trying to ignite a spark they were too slow to fire.

Ahead of him he saw a small grouping of buildings, askew huts with tin roofs. A thin trace of smoke rose from a hole, and he walked toward the largest hut from which that plume curled. A low humming that emanated through the battered screen door stopped when he opened it. A small boy began to silently cry when he saw Allan, turning his face against his father's legs. The father put his hand on the boy's head and the boy turned around, leaning back against his father, his arms bent behind him, clasped around his father's legs. The father looked at Allan and said "Hello" in English, a slight accent in the voice that Allan couldn't place. "My father told me that you'd be coming." The boy began to cry again, making no sound. The boy looked at Allan with terror in his eyes, as if his arrival had long been feared, and fearing it so long had done nothing to ease the horror of the moment occurring. The boy's father looked at Allan directly and without emotion, numb to anything but the fact that this strange man stood in this room with them, that he was undeniable, and that the story his own father had told him for so long was a true story, had always been true, despite the years of scoffing at his father's words, of dismissing his father's work as a fool's myth, a trickster's occupation, remnant of a dying cul-

ture, nostalgia for stories in which magic solved the problem of sickness, the problem of the world; this man looked at Allan with eyes that could not deny what they could not believe.

An old man lay in a bed, thin arm on top of the haphazard sheet, naked foot exposed. The old man shivered beneath the cloth. "He's cold," Allan said. "No," the man said, "he's not cold." A single layer of gauze covered the old man's eyes, through which, as through a veil, his eyes could still be seen. "He complained about the light," the man said. "His eyes are always wide now. For him it is always dark and his eyes are wide."

Allan took the scroll out of his bag. The man looked at him; he never seemed to blink. "Go ahead," he said, "he knows why you are here."

"Do you sing like your father?" Allan asked.

"It is a language I refused to learn, a superstitious language. I am a man of science, and I left this island to learn the real names of things. I am here now only because my father is dying, and to watch as his words don't save him."

"The words will save him. I've come here because—"

"It does not matter to me why you've come. My father said you would. He told me he must see you. He is about to die, and what you are about to do will be what kills him. He has no strength left, not even for this sham."

"You will see," Allan said, "that you are wrong." He unrolled the scroll, and began to sing the song he taught himself. The first syllable extended into a sustained note growing higher and higher in pitch, and it unlocked in Allan's mind, as he had come to expect and withstand, the most intimate mem-

ories of his wife, her hair spread across her pillow, the snail's track of her eyes in bliss, memories he had learned not to ignore but to use as the entrance into the next syllable, the next word's low note in which memory ceased. At the sound the old man stopped shaking and, as Allan knew he would, began to sing the song below the song, the drone without which the melody had no power. Allan felt beneath his feet the floor sag, as if the song he sang were weighing him down, or as if he and the old man were singing the earth open, singing the solid earth into liquid, singing slowly earth into ocean, into which Allan slowly sank, caught in the midst of the transformation he himself sang. He saw through his eyes and behind his eyes, a double-vision—saw the bed of the old man beginning to rise above him, saw the old man's son staring down at him, saw the boy run crying from the room; and he saw, too, his own son at home, reading a letter on his bed; he saw his wife just after she died, and his baby daughter in his arms; he saw an apple tree in full bloom floating in the air, but the air wasn't air; he saw the white-blossoming apple tree in full bloom floating in the water; he saw a pocket watch on which a fox in amateur hand had been etched on the metal falling through the water, its chain a straight line above it like the tail of a comet; he saw a blue umbrella open; and swimming between them all, lazy, omnipotent, a white whale with a black cord wrapped in coils around its body.

And then the vision stopped, and then the floor was a tight circle around his waist, and Allan looked up, still holding the note in his mouth, still singing the word, a small word, singing "and." He was singing "and," a word of great complexity in the song, the word that refuses any other word's desire to be unconnected, to be alone. The old man bolted upright in his bed, sweat trickling down his face. His eyes were wide open and yet unstaring behind the gauze, roving around, as if looking for something missing, some object of which he must gain hold.

Allan could not help himself. He broke the song in order to ask in the song's language what he must do. *What must I do? The old man turned his head slowly over, tilted it slowly down, and looked at Allan. He understood Allan's words. What must I do? Teach me.* The old man spoke. His son watched; listened, shook slowly his head no. The old man spoke but Allan could understand none of his words. *What must I do?* Allan looked below him and, as if peering through depths of clear water he saw two shapes rising toward him, one embraced or within the other. *What must I do?* And the old man answered, yelled his answer in rhythmic chants, words Allan could not understand but could almost recognize, the words of the scroll but words that in the old singer's mouth took on a different shape so that Allan did not know how to grasp them, to fit them into understanding. The old man spoke more emphatically, gesticulating wildly the same spiraling motion over and over; and then he stopped, stopped talking and stopped his arms from gesturing. He looked at Allan directly, eyes piercing behind their veil, and in perfect English the old man said, "Why can't you hear me?" Allan looked below him and saw the two shapes rising, and above them, the water growing dark, becoming solid. In horror, Allan thought he heard knocking beneath the floor that now was only floor, was ocean no longer, but there was no knocking, there was only the *thud of the old man falling out of bed to the ground.*

"It is as I told you it would be," the son said. He took a long while to bend down to his father. "And now you should go. That was not your song to sing. You should have known that. It's not anyone's song to sing. It's a bauble, a plaything. A story for fools told by fools." He put his hand on his father's neck; put his open hand in front of his father's mouth. "And now this fool—" and the man stopped speaking, stood up, and turned his face away to the wall.

The stupid moon shone through the window. I don't know why that thought was my thought as I put down my pen, as I turned the pages over, as I turned my father over in my mind, as I put my father away, as I put him down.

The stupid moon shone through the window.

CHAPTER 7

my father alone in the top of a tree

all alone in the top of the tree singing

he is not calling to me my name
he is not singing to me

he's singing the names I've forgotten
the names I've never known

by his voice I find him singing
alone in the top of the tree

his feet hang down like fruit
in the blossoms the bare soles of his feet

it is me father it is me
this is the endless song I sing

it is me father it is
no song

I am no song but my father hears me

he throws down to me fruit after fruit

his song sings of what it is I have forgotten

he tells me to eat and I'll remember

eat

I pick up fruit after small fruit
but I eat none I can't eat I won't eat none

each is an eye my father throws down his eyes
on me they fall down as he sings

my father throws down his eyes

then I realize these fruit are his eyes
these fruit are his eyes

and I cannot see him

✻

I woke to the alarm. Pirates off the Barbary Coast.

I walked downstairs. I made my cup of coffee. I went
to the study. I had turned the postcard over so I could
not see those stars. There was the severed poet's head. It
was turned away—of course, this was coincidence—
from the stack of pages next to it. I thought to myself,
It's done. Something was missing, I could feel it but I
couldn't name it. There sat the green book on its shelf. I
walked to the window and stared out. Almost all the

leaves had fallen from the poplar, pale yellow pocked with brown spots. A fox ran across the yard in the sickly morning light. It kept looking back behind it even as it sped forward, pursued even though nothing chased it. At least, nothing I could see. I heard a ticking from my desk, and, opening the drawer, next to the letter opener, the old pocket watch Lydia bought me, the watch that had never worked, that never would work, was ticking, but no hands moved. I picked it up and the ticking stopped.

Time passed.

Some amount of time. It always passes. Nothing need mark it. It need not be counted.

Time passes. It passed.

I moved inside of it, time, as it passed. I got dressed. I rubbed the pomade into my hands, sandalwood a scent in the air, and put my hands through my hair. I gathered my books and papers. I took the green book from its shelf and put it in my bag. I closed the door behind me and left for school. I walked down the path I always walked down, the path I'm always walking down, always.

I looked behind me. There it was, as it always was. Nothing following me.

⚹

Ishmael was waiting for me by my office door. "Hello, Professor."

Seeing him there, seeing in his face his patience and his expectation—it felt like a hammer pressing down on my chest. I saw him and felt in me the weight of all I should ask him but could not, would not ask, about his mother, about what happened to her, how she died—I wanted to ask if his mother ever discovered her world, her other worlds, the math that proved it, or if he found her too at times at the dinner table drawing circles one on top of another in reverie or mindless repetition—about his childhood, about what he knew of his father, what he knew about me. *Me.* That one syllable struck my mind as a hammer strikes stained glass. Once again—I feared it because I felt so certain of it— I was making up the story I wanted to be true, refusing to let shatter what in my life had already shattered. I looked at Ishmael. I felt him to be a wonderful young man. I took pride in him. I would be proud to have him as a son. And his eyes, that look in his eyes, as in my own eyes—that proved enough for me to put him to work in my imagination gluing the shards back together, one by one, until the picture again was whole in its panels: a man and a woman and a child through which the light gains color as it shines. I need to put that world away, I thought. I need to bury the dead. But I only turned the key in the lock, opened my office door, and said, "Come in, Ishmael. And please, don't call me Professor; it makes me feel older than I am. *Professor*—it's a word that conjures pontificating shades. Daniel is just fine."

Ishmael sat down while I emptied my bag of books and notes. I pulled out the green book and held it for a moment, felt again how it seemed denser than it should be, weighed somehow more than it should, but also felt how the stories inside it had filled my young head with fantasies that had not yet released me from the magic lantern spinning its light and shadows onto the wall in my mind. Worlds that weighed nothing at all. I put the book on the desk between us.

"What is it?" Ishmael asked, looking down at the book.

"An old book I read as a child. *Wonders and Tales*. I borrowed it from the Old Library a number of months ago, and realized I should return it. It is a book, I think, of some value." I paused, and clarified. "Monetary value." I picked up the book. "Why don't we return it now? Would you mind joining me? Can we talk about your concerns as we walk?"

"Sure," Ishmael said. We stood up together and walked out the door. "Do you need to close it?" Ishmael asked, noticing I hadn't pulled the door closed behind us.

"No. Maybe I'll get lucky and someone will steal everything." I heard myself as Ishmael must hear me. "I'm sorry. I'm sounding rather jaded today." We walked down the stairs and out the heavy wooden doors of Trillbyrne Hall. "What did you want to talk about?"

Ishmael hesitated. "Well, um—the paper, I guess. I still don't know what to write about. I have lots of thoughts, really. I've taken notes. I've written ideas on little cards. I've pinned the cards to my wall and drawn lines between them to see how they connect. But I can always see they could make another shape, you know? That it's arbitrary. That I'm just forcing them into something I recognize but there isn't any inherent connection. I'm just playing—"

"You're drawing lines between the stars—consideration, constellation—"

"Yes. I guess. But it's awful, and I can't write a thing."

We walked across the lawn, kicking leaves with every step; a raucous, mournful sound. Discord of trespass. Ishmael slowed his pace, looking down at the leaves as he kicked them. "But I actually came by to apologize for my behavior in yesterday's class." He stopped walking and looked at me. "I get emotional sometimes . . . when something makes me remember my mom."

The dead don't stay buried, I thought. Stone's weight of the green book in my hand. "Tell me about her," I said. It felt to me as if the words had uttered themselves, as if I had withdrawn and taken a seat deep within myself, to listen without the questionable problem of me always being myself.

"She was a weaver."

"Was she?" in too quick a response, both horrified and horrifically relieved that all my thoughts were wrong. That this boy was my student, nothing more. It released something in me. Some rope or chain or thread or string I'd been gripping tightly—so tightly I didn't know I was doing it—came loose, or my hand of its own tiredness unclenched. But what that line attached to did not fall when I let it go, it rose, I felt it rise above me, the life that had almost been mine, I felt it rise above me as I felt myself fall, no real falling, a worse one, as if gravity became suddenly more than a natural law and became instead a spiritual one. I mean to say something in me fell, and what fell in me was me.

"Well, she became a weaver. She had been a physicist. An astronomer. She studied other worlds, the possibility of other worlds."

"No—" I heard my voice speak itself.

"Yes," Ishmael said. He looked at me with surprise, almost amusement, at the vehemence of my reaction. "She told me that in the end they were the same thing—weaving and worlds. I don't think I yet understand what she meant. My favorite memories of her are sitting on the floor by her as she threw the shuttle across the warp and pushed the weft together. You wouldn't think it, but it's a deafening noise. A kind of music, like—" we started walking again, "like feet stepping through leaves. Hours would pass. It would hypnotize me—it really would—watching her take a single thread of a single color and make it into a pattern—"

"Into a world—"

"Yes. I guess that's right, Professor. I mean, Daniel. A world." The Old Library loomed, its tower seeming to lean over us, either to collapse us in its rubble, or to shepherd us inside. "She would have liked to hear you say that. She would have liked you, I think."

"How—" I felt the color drain from my face, felt ashen, "How did she die?"

"Cancer."

"I'm sorry, Ishmael." I put my hand on his shoulder. I had never touched him before. He felt my hand shaking.

"Are you O.K., Daniel?"

I turned my head away so that I wouldn't cry. Seeing him would make me cry. But I kept my hand on his shoulder. "So it's your father that raised you?"

"No—." Ishmael's voice grew dim. "I don't know who my father is. My mother said he was a writer. I never felt I could ask."

"You are an orphan."

"I am. I guess so." He frowned; his chin quivered.

"I'm sorry, Ishmael." I said, and looked at him as I spoke. I took my hand from his shoulder. "I'm sorry."

"It's not your fault, Professor."

Ishmael walked up the steps and opened the doors, and I followed him, and we both went in.

The bottom floor had not changed since Olin and I stole in those months before. The bookshelves like cripples leaning against each other, pausing on the long walk home. Sheets gathering the dust that should fall on the unused tables. The broken lamp. We started up the stairs. The green book grew heavier and heavier in my hand, gathering gravity inside itself, a dense star.

"There's a story I remember, Ishmael. I read it in this book when I was a boy." I gave him the book to carry.

"There was once was an old woman, a magical woman, who could sing songs, and everything she sang about came true. When she was hungry, she sang a song of carrots and potatoes growing in the ground, of harvesting them, of cooking them in the pot, and at the end of the song there would be a bowl of soup steaming on her table. People in the town knew of her power, and she was not selfish. When a child was born blind the parents would bring the baby to her, and she would sing her a new pair of eyes. When the drought came she would sing rain and it would rain. She was a very old lady, and near the end of her life. She decided, when one day she was singing her house clean, hearing how hoarse her voice sounded, that she wanted to live her life over again. So she sang. She sang herself back through her own life, reversing it, sang her own grown children back into infants, back into nothing. She sang her husband out of the grave and back into the beauty of his youth; she sang herself young with him." We had come to the landing, and walked into the Old Library. Ishmael gazed around, looked at the books locked behind their glass cases, looked at the plaster ornaments circling the ceiling, looked up at Pan looking down. "She sang herself back into her own childhood; she sang the apple orchard in blossom. She sang herself back to a baby, back to a time when she had no song of her own, but could only hear the song in the air that spoke its ongoing tune. But she forgot something. Do you know what she forgot?"

Ishmael and I stood in front of the bookcase from which I'd stolen the book.

"She forgot her parents."

"Right." I looked at Ishmael. I looked at him in his eyes with my eyes. "And so this baby spoke her first words. Do you know what they were?"

"Mom. Dad."

"Right. And they appeared."

Ishmael looked at the shelf. He saw the broken pieces of the lock in the gap left by the stolen book. He looked at me. "You borrowed this book?" He pulled open the case, but I put my hand against it, against the glass. I felt the glass cool against my fingers.

"I think I might borrow it a while longer," I said. "Maybe you should borrow it from me."

Ishmael closed the glass case, and we walked down the stairs and out the building, hurrying so as not to be late for class.

CHAPTER 8

EVERY HEAD TURNED TOWARD US WHEN WE ENTERED the room.

Ishmael took his seat, and I took mine.

"I've been thinking about the essay assignment," I said. "I know some of you have been having a difficult time coming up with something to write. It's strange material we're reading. Myth and fairy tales, stories of wonder and magic, darkness and light, shadows and bodies. It is like entering a new world, these stories. Paying attention to them initiates you in things that shouldn't be real, shouldn't feel real—monsters and heroes, simpletons and princesses, wise women and witches. Analyzing wonder feels like writing an argumentative essay about your lover proving you love her. It's, um, untoward, impolite, something. And of course, this is college, in which no one tells you that learning how to think is a lesson in betrayal." I couldn't tell if I made any sense to the class. Not so sure I made sense to myself. No one nodded his head; no one took notes. "So, I decided all of you should have a different option—one that doesn't ask you to betray the work you've done, but asks you to do it further." I glanced at Ishmael. I thought to myself, *There he is.* "There's a story my father used to tell me. He told it to me every night before bed. It's a story—

maybe the only one—I know word for word. It doesn't begin 'Once upon a time,' but let the phrase linger as if already spoken in your ear.

"After the giant removed his heart and buried it in the ground his eyes gradually grew smaller and smaller until he seemed to have no eyes at all. He did still have eyes, but they were no larger than pinpricks, smaller than the eyes of a mole, as small as a spider's eyes, and let in so little light that the giant was mostly blind. He couldn't tell when it was night or day and so he stopped sleeping. He couldn't walk without running into trees or tripping over ridges or falling down in rivers. He just sat down and didn't move. He sat so long that moss grew on him. Grass grew on the moss. Trees in the grass: an aspen grove. He seemed dead but he was not dead. When the wind pushed through the aspen and the leaves made a riverlike music the giant would hear it, some nerve would awaken, and though he had no heart, from his pinprick eyes a tear would fall, so thin and meager that the wind that caused it would also take it away. People who passed the giant thought he was only a hill whose stony crest was pink as skin. Their parents and their parent's parents had walked by the hill many times, had carted their goods down the road that curved around the giant, and in all their memory that hill had only ever been a hill. But the birds knew. Whether they could hear his breath, or feel the slightest twitches of muscles that sometimes sent a leaf spiraling down from a branch in midsummer, or sense beneath his head the hum of his thinking, no one can say—but there were no nests in the aspen trees. But the people didn't notice this either. To the sudden absence of birdsong at the hill when they walked past it the people all were deaf.

"It was at the foot of this hill that the people of the village built their schoolhouse."

I stopped speaking. I stopped because the story stopped.

"And?—" said anonymously.

"And that's all there is. My father never finished the story. He said he didn't know the end. So, for those of you who would like a different assignment, it is this: Finish the tale."

I heard a noise in the room as of someone mockingly scoffing. Otherwise, the class was silent, unmoving.

"Go ahead," I said. "You all can leave. Class is dismissed."

"But there's still an hour left."

"Well, enjoy the extra time. The story's been told, so class is over."

Everyone left. I watched Ishmael walk away, green book held in his hand.

✳

I went home, too.

I opened the door my father had opened. I wiped the thin line of dust off the top of the frame in which my mother blushed. I walked down the hallway my father walked down, walked into the study that had been his study. I sat down in the chair in the room whose walls once vibrated with his voice, his song; I thought I could hear in the air a low hum as if the walls were vibrating still.

I turned the postcard over. Underneath Orpheus's severed head three stars darkly shone. I was one of those stars. My son was another. And the third, Lydia—whose light still cut across infinite distance though its source long ago had been expired.

The finished novel thick in the middle of the desk— in it I wrote my father's cenotaph. Wrote his failure. Buried him in it. Buried him in the names.

I looked at the thick stack of pages, and I felt ashamed.

I turned the title page over, and began to read. *I learned to be a quiet child.* I read the sentence, and then I crossed it out.

~~*I learned to be a quiet child.*~~

I read the next sentence, and crossed it out, too. And I kept reading, sentence by sentence, crossing each one out. I had, I thought, woven it wrongly—all of it.

The hours passed. The sun set. Night's dark line crossed out the day. My fingertips hurt from holding the pen, my thumb indented, thumbprint erased.

I thought I could hear it, as I dragged my pen across the words I read. I thought I could hear the earth rolling in its rut. They sound the same. A starling sang its mimic-song: creak of a door closing, creak of an old branch in the wind, stolen notes of the cardinal's crystalline call. The starlings' breasts mottled with stars, pale dots against the metallic black sheen of feathers—I watched them in the moonlight, stalking through the grass, yellow beaks cracked open.

I read the end of the last sentence: *the man stopped speaking, stood up, and turned his face away to the wall.*

How had I become that man?

I crossed it out: ~~the man stopped speaking, stood up, and turned his face away to the wall~~.

The pages littered the floor. My finger and thumb throbbed, ached. I could feel the bones inside them.

The only page left on the desk was the title page, *An Impenetrable Screen of Purest Sky* written in red ink across a musical staff. I turned the page over, the dark lines of the musical staff faint but still visible.

I picked up my pen.

When my mother and sister died, my father learned to sing.

He learned the words to a heroic song, and when he sang he became a hero.

He travelled by ship to an island where an old man helped him sing.

My father and the old man sang together this heroic song.

The song opened a door between our world and another, the world where the dead wait, looking always up into the air above them. The song changed the floor into ocean, and my father swam down, singing as he swam, never taking a breath, to the ocean's bottom.

There he stood and peered into a vast chasm. He saw the vertebrae of a giant whale, and he saw that whale's giant jaws. And sitting in those jaws he saw his wife, and in his wife's arms, his baby daughter.

He sang to them and they heard his song. They swam up to him, following him as he sang, following him up through the sea, which they mistook for air; they followed his song whose words bubbled upward. My father—he never looked back. He only sang.

And then the ocean became a floor underneath his feet. Then my father stopped singing, and the old man stopped singing, too. Then his baby daughter took a breath and cried. Father turned around, just then he turned around, and there in his eyes were his wife and child.

The old man said, You must forget this song.

My father said, It is forgotten.

Some time passed, and that time was silent.

There was a knock on my door. I was a little boy, not a man. I sat on my bed reading my father's letters when I heard a knock on my door. And when I opened it my mother knelt down before me, her arms open, her face no longer looking down. Behind her stood my father, humming quietly to the baby to keep her calm, to keep her calm as she drifted off to that other world of dreams and danger, to calm her as she drifted off to sleep.

And then I put the pen down. I rested it on the page.

I went upstairs, and to drift off to that other world of dreams and danger, to drift off to sleep.

CHAPTER 9

I woke up late. Such a simple sentence. i woke up late and went to school.

My office door stood wide open. I walked in. Nothing was missing.

On my desk, in the very middle of it, some pages stapled together. I sat down on my desk and picked it up. Handwritten at the top in blue ink: *Here is my paper—Ishmael.*

The children who sat in the desks in that school forgot everything as soon as they learned it. In the afternoons the hill's giant shadow fell over the school—a heartless shadow—and the morning's lessons, what two apples added to two apples equals, what the names of the shapes on the map were, all disappeared. The teacher didn't notice that anything was wrong, for she would forget herself what she taught.

When the children went home they were quieter than when they left. It was a quiet their parents appreciated, which made them quiet as well.

The children would go to school and forget more and more of what they had known of the world.

Many things struck them all as beautiful, the teacher and the students. A golden butterfly flew in the open window and fluttered around the room in widening circles, a butterfly that seemed to glow. It landed on the finger of one boy who held his finger out, but the glow dimmed, and the butterfly flew weakly away.

Eventually there were no words left that any of the children could remember, and their parents remembered only a few— their child's name, perhaps, or perhaps their own.

One day, before the school bell rang, the children wandered out of the schoolhouse. They wandered out only because the door had been left open. They walked past their parents even as their parents called out their names. They had no names they knew. Each child wandered off in his or her own direction, they didn't know to follow each other.

The boy on whose finger the butterfly had landed walked through a field of goldenrod. Bees as big as thumbs hummed as they worked, and the boy heard this, and he hummed too. He hummed as he wandered through the field.

He walked across the field and into the woods where the jack-in-the-pulpit grows. The forest was dark but the boy had forgotten how to be afraid.

He saw a little glow shining from a hole in the ground and he walked over to it and looked in. There in the bottom of it was the golden butterfly glowing, but when the boy reached down to touch it, it flew up beyond his reach, and circled in widening circles around him.

A fragment of the butterfly's wing had broken off, and glowed golden in the dirt. The boy reached for it but it always seemed below his grasp, so that without knowing he was doing so, the boy dug the hole deeper, dug until he was standing inside the hole he was digging, and then the fragment was in his hand,

and he dug no more. The glow went out as soon as he held it. But something else glowed, a pale white glow. The boy bent down and picked up a rock. It was a white rock, a crystal rock, a quartz. It felt warm in the boy's hand, and gently pulsed. The boy closed his hand around it and felt it beat warmly in his hand.

The butterfly ceased its circling and landed on the boy's shoulder. He looked at it, and when it flew away, he followed it. He climbed out the hole with rock in hand and followed its golden light through the dark woods, followed it through the field of goldenrod where the bees slept inside their blooms. He followed it all the way to his school, and up the hill that stood next to the school. The sun was rising, but the boy didn't know the difference between night and day. He followed the butterfly up the hill to a little spring, a little spring in the middle of a little pond. The butterfly dipped down and touched the water, flew up and over to the boy and gently touched his hand that held the beating rock. The butterfly repeated this over and over again, until a dim thought grew bright in the forgetful boy's head.

The boy threw the stone into the pond, into the spring, and it disappeared with a splash. The butterfly flew in front of the boy's face and glowed so brightly the boy had to close his eyes. He heard himself say, "Too bright." These are the first words the boy remembers ever saying.

Somewhere the hill that was a giant opened his eyes, and his eyes grew wider. He didn't stand up, he didn't wander off. The giant only opened his eyes and watched. He saw the schoolhouse beside him. He felt the boy walking down his back.

At every step the boy remembered another word, but they were dim words, unconnected to anything he saw, anything in the world. He kept repeating to himself, "and and and."

And when he had walked down the hill he found himself by habit walking home. He knew it was his home when he saw it. He knocked on the door and when the door opened he saw a man who bent down and opened his arms and looked at him.

Then the boy remembered, and he said one word. The boy said, "Father."

I put the paper down and walked to my office window.

I could see the yellow lawn and the leafless trees through the transparent reflection of my own face. Through my own face I could see the pale sky, so very pale, blank as a page, and I thought to myself, *too bright, too bright.*

"Father," I said.

And my own face said "Father" back to me.

THE END

ACKNOWLEDGMENTS & NOTES

IT HAS BEEN MY CONTINUOUS LUCK TO HAVE TWO OLD FRIENDS as primary readers for nearly every word I've written, and their attention to this book both encouraged me to keep writing it, and made it better than it would have been left to my hands alone: thank you Sally Keith and Srikanth Reddy. Much of the novel was pondered and put together while running many miles with Michael Lundblad, and his patience in listening to me talk as we trained for a marathon was an attention greatly needed, and I hope reflected in the book itself. Thank you to my father, and to Agelia Dumas, for reading drafts of the book and offering support and advice in return; thank you to my mother for the same. Thank you to Chris Fischbach and everyone at Coffee House Press. Thank you to Laird Hunt for publishing Book III, Chapter 6 in the *Denver Quarterly*. Lastly, but a circular last so that it is always also the beginning, thank you to Iris, Hana, and Kristy, who in me exert such a tow that image reverts back to substance, and that substance is home.

✴

The poet who falls into and through the volcano is in memory of Craig Arnold.

Many other books wend their way through the fabric of this one, a tribute and a study of those works and writers I most love. Readers of this book will find echoes in homage to Herman Melville, Ralph Waldo Emerson, Emily Dickinson, Marcel Proust, John Berryman, John Bunyan, T. S. Eliot, Henry David Thoreau, William Blake, Nathaniel Hawthorne, George MacDonald, Walter Benjamin, Gerard Manley Hopkins, William Faulkner, and Virginia Woolf, among others.

COLOPHON

An Impenetrable Screen of Purest Sky
was designed at Coffee House Press,
in the historic Grain Belt Brewery's
Bottling House near downtown Minneapolis.
The text is set in Bembo.

COFFEE HOUSE PRESS

The mission of Coffee House Press is to publish exciting, vital, and enduring authors of our time; to delight and inspire readers; to contribute to the cultural life of our community; and to enrich our literary heritage. By building on the best traditions of publishing and the book arts, we produce books that celebrate imagination, innovation in the craft of writing, and the many authentic voices of the American experience.

FUNDER ACKNOWLEDGMENTS

COFFEE HOUSE PRESS is an independent, nonprofit literary publisher. Our books are made possible through the generous support of grants and gifts from many foundations, corporate giving programs, state and federal support, and through donations from individuals who believe in the transformational power of literature. Coffee House Press receives major operating support from Amazon, the Bush Foundation, the Jerome Foundation, the McKnight Foundation, from the National Endowment for the Arts—a federal agency, from Target, and in part from a grant provided by the Minnesota State Arts Board through an appropriation by the Minnesota State Legislature from the State's general fund and its arts and cultural heritage fund with money from the vote of the people of Minnesota on November 4, 2008, and a grant from the Wells Fargo Foundation of Minnesota. Coffee House also receives support from: several anonymous donors; Suzanne Allen; Elmer L. and Eleanor J. Andersen Foundation; Around Town Agency; Patricia Beithon; Bill Berkson; the E. Thomas Binger and Rebecca Rand Fund of the Minneapolis Foundation; the Patrick and Aimee Butler Family Foundation; the Buuck Family Foundation, Ruth Dayton;

Dorsey & Whitney, LLP; Mary Ebert and Paul Stembler; Chris Fischbach and Katie Dublinski; Fredrikson & Byron, P.A.; Sally French; Anselm Hollo and Jane Dalrymple-Hollo; Jeffrey Hom; Carl and Heidi Horsch; Kenneth Kahn; Alex and Ada Katz; Stephen and Isabel Keating; the Kenneth Koch Literary Estate; Kathy and Dean Koutsky; the Lenfestey Family Foundation; Carol and Aaron Mack; Mary McDermid; Sjur Midness and Briar Andresen; the Nash Foundation; the Rehael Fund of the Minneapolis Foundation; Schwegman, Lundberg & Woessner, P.A.; Kiki Smith; Jeffrey Sugerman and Sarah Schultz; Patricia Tilton; the Archie D. & Bertha H. Walker Foundation; Stu Wilson and Mel Barker; the Woessner Freeman Family Foundation; Margaret and Angus Wurtele; and many other generous individual donors.

   amazon.com

To you and our many readers across the country, we send our thanks for your continuing support.